Land of Seagull and Fox

LAND of
SEAGULL and FOX
Folk Tales of Vietnam

collected and retold by **Ruth Q. Sun**

illustrations by HO THANH DUC

A WEATHERMARK EDITION

CHARLES E. TUTTLE COMPANY : *Rutland, Vermont*

Perhaps four thousand years ago--for who can be sure about legends?--a lineal descendant of one of the great emperors of Chinese antiquity is said to have made a tour to the south, into the land known today as Vietnam. There he met a Tien or heavenly spirit so beautiful as to steal the breath, and of their union was born a son who came in time to reign over the land, then known as

Xich Quy, the Land of the Red Devils. This son in turn married the daughter of the God of the Sea, and their son was Lac Long or Fox Dragon, who also ruled the land until he retired to the Palace of the Sea. But another emperor of China coveted this fair land, and Fox Dragon had to return to its defense. Repelling the Chinese invaders, he later took to wife the mountain spirit Au Co, whose name means Seagull Maiden, and she bore him one hundred sons at a single time. When the time came for parting, they divided their sons equally, and the father took fifty to live with him in the Palace of the Sea, while the mother took the other fifty to live with her in the high mountains. These were the ancestors of the Vietnamese of today, so the story goes, and in honor of their parents they changed the name of their country from the Land of the Red Devils to the Land of Seagull and Fox. . . .

First U.S. edition, 1967
Copyright in Japan, 1966
by John Weatherhill, Inc.
All rights reserved
Printed in Japan
LCC Card No. 67–23010

Distributed in Japan by
JOHN WEATHERHILL, INC., Tokyo
and in the rest of the world by
CHARLES E. TUTTLE CO., INC., Rutland, Vermont
with representation on the Continent by
BOXERBOOKS, INC., *Zurich*
in the British Isles by
PRENTICE-HALL INTERNATIONAL, INC., *London*
in Australasia by
PAUL FLESCH & CO., PTY. LTD., *Melbourne*
and in Canada by
m. g. hurtig, ltd., *Edmonton*

To my
Vietnamese
students
in gratitude,
in affection,
in remembrance

through times of
uncertainty, doubt,
and occasional fear
we shared language,
laughter, lore,
literature,
love

Contents

Foreword

VIETNAM IS NOT ONLY the beautiful land of "dragons and immortal fairies." It is also a nation made up of human beings—farmers, artisans, merchants, soldiers, scholars, poets. Even most of the village gods were at one time ordinary persons who have been deified because of their bravery in leading the people against aggressors from the north or because they taught their fellow villagers some useful new trade or technique. The folk literature of Vietnam, consisting of proverbs and sayings, riddles and tales, likewise emphasizes the people of the land—gods and humans, commoners and kings, heroes and villains. These tales that are handed down from generation to generation—told by innumerable grandmothers to their many grandchildren—make up a wealthy treasure of Vietnamese folklore. As a son of Vietnam responsible for cultural affairs to the Ministry of Education, I take pleasure in introducing to our English-reading friends this new collection of Vietnamese folk tales retold by a most sympathetic student of Asian culture.

Ruth Sun, who has lived in Asia for a number of years and has a special interest in Asian literature, lent valuable assistance as a Fulbright Lecturer on the Faculty of Letters at the University of Saigon during the academic year 1964–65. Her choice of stories, like her delightful English style, could not be happier. Her endeavor is especially laudable at a time when banner headlines and sensational newsreels seem to make people from afar lose sight of one important aspect of Vietnamese life— the tender, the romantic, the wonder-filled—that is so well exhibited in these stories.

May many friends of Vietnam from the "four seas" enjoy these stories and, through them, gain deeper insight into the psychology of the valiant people of Vietnam, whose destiny has been a constant struggle against the totalitarian forces that would enslave this land, a centuries-old struggle for independence—national and individual, political and moral. May other students of Vietnam emulate Mrs. Sun and make similar efforts to interpret Vietnamese life and thought to the world. Sympathy like this makes warm the heart and is without price.

Saigon, 1966   NGUYEN DINH HOA
Director of Cultural Affairs
Ministry of Education
Republic of Vietnam

Introduction

"THE VIETNAMESE LIVE on rice and legends and myths," so runs an ancient saying from an incredibly lovely, incredibly beset land. Perhaps three words should now be added to the proverb: "... and on hope," in recognition of a new awakening in the midst of struggle.

Who are these people? Although in recent years modern Vietnam has been a focus of world interest, and discord, many Westerners have not had too clear a notion of exactly where the country is nor, more important, who its people are. Perhaps this collection of their folk tales can serve in a sense as introduction.

Certainly folklore is revealing of a people's basic beliefs and yearnings, of their imaginative flights from harsh reality and of their deepest desires, of their search for the consolation of reliance upon some larger, external force, of their desire to bequeath their sense of values to their children and their children's children. As such, a nation's folk tales have significance even beyond their sheer storytelling beauty.

But there is another side to the coin. At the same time that folk tales express a people's unique qualities, they also partake of the universal, reflecting man's earliest interpretation of his own surroundings and of the basic human plight. Thus it is that many lands have developed, almost independently of each other, tales of striking similarity. It is not surprising that many of the Vietnamese tales should have earlier Chinese counterparts: Vietnamese culture is essentially an offshoot of the parent Chinese culture. But the reader will also find here echoes of Excalibur, of Cinderella, of Rip van Winkle, of tales from many lands. So perhaps as we read these tales and learn something about the Vietnamese we are also learning something about man himself, about ourselves.

❖   ❖   ❖

In making this collection I have tried to choose those tales that seem to me most representative of the genre, most revealing of Vietnamese

11

ways of thought, and most interesting for Western readers. Assistance has come from many sources, most particularly from my students at the University of Saigon, to all of whom these tales, in some one or other of their many versions, are a familiar heritage. I am also indebted to the pioneering work of a number of scholars and folklorists, especially to Mr. Pham Duy Khiem, whose versions of many of the tales were published at Hanoi in 1943 and at Paris in 1951 under the title *Légendes des terres sereines,* and to Mrs. Bach Lan, whose *Vietnamese Legends* was published at Saigon in 1957. The story of the fisherman Le Loi and its accompanying verse, which conclude this Introduction, come from Mr. Do Van Minh's *Viet Nam: Where East and West Meet.*

My debt to Mr. Pham is especially great in those stories where I have closely followed his felicitous French versions, including also his comments on the relationships between the ancient stories and present-day Vietnam, as in "The Supernatural Crossbow," "The Beginning of Good Conversation" ("The Betel and the Areca" in his version), "The Butterfly in the Granary," "The Young Wife of Nam Xuong," "The Mountain of Hope," and "The Encounter with Death" ("Trang Tu and the Death of His Wife"). My thanks both to him and his French publishers, Mercure de France, for their kind permission to use his material.

In my retellings of these tales I have attempted to retain the flavor of the originals while blending the various sources in a new way. My greatest debt of all is, of course, to the people of Vietnam, from whose folk genius all the stories ultimately derive.

My expressions of gratitude would not be complete without a word of special appreciation to the artist, Mr. Ho Thanh Duc, of Saigon, whose sensitive pen-and-ink interpretations underline the Vietnamese spirit of the stories; to Miss Phung Thi Luong Chau, who provided patient and efficient liaison between artist and writer; to Mr. Meredith Weatherby, most helpful of editors; and finally, to my husband, Norman Sun, who endured with graceful forbearance the prolonged process of stitching together a book.

✦   ✦   ✦

Like Dr. Nguyen in his kind Foreword, the Vietnamese have sometimes referred to themselves as "Sons of the Dragons, Grandsons of the Spirits." This is by way of reference to their legendary past, kept alive among them by their rich store of myths and marvelous tales, in so many of which there appear dragons and the supernatural beings called spirits or immortals or, in Vietnamese, Tien.

The basic Vietnamese legend, one of whose many versions has been summarized on the title page, is a cosmic myth of Chinese origin. Like the Japanese myth of Izanagi and Izanami, it establishes a divine beginning for the Vietnamese people, for the story has it that they originated from an encounter, one night thousands of years ago, between the Dragon King Lac Long and the Fairy Queen Au Co. Of the hundred children resulting from this union, half dwelt in the mountains with their mother, and the other half resided with their father at the seashore, in the area termed the "cradle of modern Vietnam." This legend is embodied in an early name of the country, Au Lac, formed of a syllable each from the names of the Dragon King and the Fairy Queen and written with two Chinese characters meaning "seagull" and "fox."

Both the legend and the name are significant. According to the historian D. G. E. Hall, writing in his *History of Southeast Asia,* they emphasize "the fact that all major migrations into the Indo-Chinese peninsula came from the north, from the mountains (China and Tibet), descending into the valleys to conflict with ethnic peoples. Thus there developed a permanent antagonism between the people of the mountains and those of the plains and borderlands of the sea. And this antagonism is the basic theme of the myths surrounding the legendary origin of the Kingdom of Van Lang and Au Lac, a theme that recurs in the folklore of all Southeast Asian peoples. They all share a mythology imbued with a cosmological dualism of mountain versus sea." Or, as the Chinese poet-priest Chien Chen expressed the thought some twelve hundred years ago:

> Mountains and rivers divide region from region;
> But the wind and the moon are in the same sky. . . .

This dualism remains in the legends as, at a more literal level, the stories also reflect the vast Vietnamese cultural heritage from the great northern neighbor, China. Essentially, the culture of Vietnam is a Chinese culture, taken over during the thousand years of Chinese domination which began when the Chinese overlords were enjoying the sophisticated civilization of the Han dynasty, while the Vietnamese were just entering the Bronze Age. As a result of this protracted contact, Vietnamese culture is basically Confucian, and most apparent in the stories are the Confucian precepts of filial piety, loyalty to ruler, importance of the son, resignation of women, and properly defined human relationships at all levels of the social structure. Evident too is the influence of Taoism, with its thin line of demarcation between being and non-being and its strong identification of the individual with the world of nature. Also present is the strong influence of Buddhism. Just as an earlier animism left a tradition of spirits intervening in worldly affairs, so from Buddhism did the Vietnamese acquire an attitude of passivity and acceptance of suffering and death.

With a long history of antagonism toward China, despite these strong cultural ties, the Vietnamese would prefer to recall their legendary past in terms of the tale of the lovely "one-pillar pagoda" which still stands at Hanoi, a red-coral jewel reflected in a jade-green lake. The beautiful structure has long been cherished by the Vietnamese because it reminds them of the story of Le Loi, the fisherman who became a symbol of Vietnam's long struggle for independence when he led a successful revolt against domination by the Chinese—after they had renamed the country Annam, the "Pacified South," a name, incidentally, by which the country is still frequently called. Here is his story:

One day Le Loi was casting his nets into the sea as usual. But when he pulled them out they contained, not the fish he expected, but a gleaming sword. Interpreting this as a divine command, Le Loi raised a band of warriors and led them in a long, hard, but ultimately successful fight against the northern aggressor. With victory won, the grateful fisherman-general, his magic sword at his waist, offered sacrifice to the spirit of the waters. But as he bowed low before the altar, his miraculous sword sprang from its scabbard and leaped like lightning into the sky. There it was transformed into a blue dragon that whirled among the clouds, roaring thunder and breathing flame and smoke. Then it suddenly plunged into the lake far below. At that exact moment there sprang up the lovely little red pagoda that has stood as a shining symbol in that spot ever since.

And ever since that fabled day according to the Vietnamese poet Doan Quan Tan, the people of Vietnam have been confident of their national destiny, for the avenging dragon still waits beneath the lake's limpid waters, making sure that the ancient enemy, who was once overcome by Le Loi with the help of the gods, can never again rule the land:

> He fled terror-stricken, the merciless oppressor.
> The slave did not bow, but rose up
> Inexorable, having borne to the beach
> The avenging sword, miraculous and flaming!

Tokyo, August, 1966   RUTH Q. SUN

A Short Chronology of Vietnamese History

(Included, in italics, are some of the various names by which the country has been called, followed by English approximations in quotation marks.)

B.C.

2879–258   Hong Bang dynasty under 18 Hung kings. *Van Lang,* "Land of Tattooed Men."

258–207   Thuc dynasty under King An Duong. *Au Lac,* "Land of Seagull and Fox."

207–111   Trieu dynasty under 5 Trieu kings. *Nam Viet,* "Viet People in the South."

HISTORIC PERIOD

B.C.–A.D.

111–937   Under Chinese domination except for short periods of independence following frequent revolts. Called by various names in the Chinese annals at different periods: *Giao Chi,* "Land of Pigeon-toed People," *Giao Chau,* "Circumscribed Land," *Van Xuan,* "Land of Ten Thousand Springs," *Da Nang,* "Clear Tributary Land," *An Nam,* "Pacified South," *Tinh Hai,* "Land of the Clear Sea."

A.D.

937–1009   Period of transition: 939–65, Ngo dynasty. 965–67, period of the Twelve Lords. 968–80, Dinh dynasty; *Dai Co Viet,* "Big Land of the Brave Viet." 980–1009, Early Le dynasty; *Dai Co Viet.*

1010–1225   Ly dynasty. *Dai Viet,* "Big Land of the Viet," and later *An Nam Quoc,* "Peaceful Southern Land."

1225–1400   Tran dynasty. *An Nam Quoc.*

15

1400–1427   Period of transition: 1400–07, Ho dynasty; *Dai Ngu,* "Peaceful Land." 1407–13, Later Tran dynasty. 1414–27, under domination of Chinese Ming dynasty.

1428–1527   Later Le dynasty. *Dai Viet,* "Big Land of the Viet."

1527–1787   Government by feudal families, nominally under the Le kings, Mac and, later, Trinh in north; Nguyen in south. First contacts with the West: Portuguese, 1535; Dutch, 1636; English, 1672; French, 1680.

1787–1802   Revolt and rule of the Tay Son brothers, terminated by reunification of country under Emperor Gia Long, Nguyen dynasty.

1802–1945   Nguyen dynasty. *Vietnam,* "Viet People of the South."

1853–1954   French influence and domination, begun in 1853 and consolidated in 1885.

1941–1945   Japanese occupation.

1946   Return of the French; beginning of warfare between French and the Viet Minh, ending in French defeat and withdrawal.

1954   Geneva Accord, dividing Vietnam at the 17th parallel.

1955   Official end of Nguyen dynasty with Emperor Bao Dai's being replaced by Ngo Dinh Diem as Chief of State.

1955–   Internal struggle between North and South Vietnam.

Note: The above information was compiled from *A Short History of Viet-Nam* by Nguyen Van Thai and Nguyen Van Mung (Times Publishing Co., Saigon, 1958) and *The Smaller Dragon: A Political History of Vietnam* by Joseph Buttinger (Praeger, New York, 1958). For information concerning the names of the country I am indebted to the eminent Confucian scholar Nguyen Xuan Chu, of Saigon.

Land of Seagull and Fox

The Well of Immortality

LONG, LONG AGO, WHEN THE world was new and fresh and everything was just beginning, men lived an easy and comfortable life, without problems at all. As a natural consequence, men became insupportably lazy. So the time came when the Creator punished them by giving them a more limited lifetime. In other words, their life span became much, much shorter than in the good old days.

But up in the heavens there was a god named Nuoc who was extremely easygoing and kind. He thought it all over for some aeons, and finally decided he would like to do something so that human life need not be quite so curtailed.

So one late-winter day this god dropped down to earth and descended to the very bottom of a deep well with magic properties. When men became aware that there was a god down at the bottom of that well, they were very curious about the situation. Eventually a huge crowd of passers-by assembled at the edge of the well. While they were all standing there, peering intently into the dark shaft, the god Nuoc called up to them, saying that those who would follow him into the well could become immortal. After their deaths they could quickly be returned to life, he said.

Well, of course everyone who heard the god's words wanted immediately to descend and receive this promised gift of immortality, all the more so when they could finally perceive, far down in the water at the bottom of the well, the miraculous, sparkling, scintillating body of the god. How they wanted to join him—but my! the water was very cold indeed. They hesitated.

After much discussion among themselves, the people compromised by dipping only their finger tips, their toes, and the top of their heads in the

19

icy water. They also drank a mouthful each. But, despite Nuoc's urgings, not one of them dared jump entirely into the well.

So from that time on, human beings have lived only one brief lifetime. But during that single lifetime their fingernails, toenails, hair, and teeth keep growing out, growing out—and their nails and hair continue to grow even after death, it is said. This is the sustained life promised by the god Nuoc. Because of man's fear of ice-cold water, only these scattered parts of the body secured a form of immortality.

The Supernatural Crossbow

THIS FAVORITE LEGEND OF VIET-
nam is recorded in the ancient
chronicles of the land:

More than two thousand and three hundred years ago, the story goes, a king of the land of the Thuc asked for the hand of a princess of the house of Hong Bang, which ruled over the realm of Van Lang, as Vietnam was then called. The marriage proposal was met with an abrupt refusal, so embittering the king that he vowed to bring about the downfall of the Hong Bang. But he died without having succeeded in carrying out his vow of hatred, thus willing the task as a legacy to his heirs. This was the origin of a protracted state of warfare between the kingdoms of Thuc and Van Lang.

For a number of years the Hong Bang emerged always victorious from the feuding. Finally, heartened by an unbroken string of military successes and confident of the protection of the divine spirits, the Hong Bang gradually relaxed their vigilance and lulled themselves into idleness and the pursuit of pleasure.

Meantime their enemy, in the person of King Thuc Phan, was undertaking extensive and meticulous preparations, and awaiting a propitious moment for the invasion of Van Lang. When the time was ripe, he crushed the army of the eighteenth Hong Bang king.

When he realized that his cause was lost, the king of Van Lang became fearfully angry. The blood vessels in his throat burst, his blood flowed in streams from his mouth, and he ran and flung himself down a deep well. Thus ended the life of the last king of a dynasty which had descended from Than Nong, one of the five great emperors of ancient China, a legendary dynasty that is said to have lasted for perhaps more than two thousand and six hundred years.

Thuc Phan reunited the two kingdoms under the name of Au Lac, and he himself took the name and title of An Duong Vuong or King An Duong. He established his capital in the territory of Phong Khe. But scarcely were the ramparts erected than a violent storm broke in the night, and they collapsed. Three times more did An Duong have the embankments reconstructed; three times more were they destroyed in a single night.

So the king then caused an altar to be erected beyond the eastern gate, and there he began to pray to the gods. On the seventh day of the third month he saw coming from the east an old man, who said to him: "You can count upon the cooperation of the Ambassador of the Limpid Waters."

Next day, very early in the morning, the king noticed an enormous golden tortoise which came from the east, moving swiftly over the surface of the water. Speaking the language of men, this tortoise explained that he had been sent as emissary by the gods. The king at once invited him into the palace, and there begged him to explain why his builders had not been able to construct the ramparts to stay.

The golden tortoise answered: "This is a land of rivers and mountains, both inhabited by spirits. It is the spirits of the mountains that are causing your ramparts to collapse. The spirits of the waters remain friendly to you."

With the advice of the golden tortoise, An Duong was then able to triumph over the sorcery of the unfriendly spirits, and he rebuilt his fortifications rapidly. They comprised three enclosures, which extended over a thousand *truong* and twisted about in such a way that they resembled a seashell or conch. So the city was called Co Loa Thanh, the City of the Seashell.

✦ ✦ ✦

When the city and its fortifications were complete, the golden tortoise took his leave of the king. The latter thanked him profusely for his assistance, led him outside the gates, and said to him: "Thanks to you this city has become powerful. But what will happen when you are gone? Shall I be able to defend it?"

The golden tortoise answered: "Fortune and misfortune depend upon the will of heaven. But if men are deserving, heaven will help them. Since you show such great confidence in me, I can make you a present which will help you. But never forget that it is your own obligation constantly to guard the security of your kingdom."

Whereupon the tortoise broke off one of his own claws and handed it to the king, saying: "Fasten this to your crossbow as a trigger. When

you go into combat, you will then be invincible. But remember your own responsibility, and be ever alert!"

Having thus spoken, the golden tortoise turned away toward the river. The king followed him with his eyes until he had entirely disappeared from view beneath the waters.

✦ ✦ ✦

At that time there was reigning in China the powerful Tan Thuy Hoang, whom the Chinese call Ch'in Shih-huang-ti or First Emperor of the Ch'in Dynasty. He had conquered all his weaker neighbors and had extended his military power as far as the South Seas. Within his own country, this great ruler had achieved unity and overthrown feudal restraints. In the same year in which he began the construction of the Great Wall, he sent his mighty forces south to attack the kingdom of Au Lac. But, led by their king with his magic crossbow, the warriors of Au Lac were able to hurl back the great Chinese armies even before they approached.

Three years later, this emperor entrusted five hundred thousand men to General Trieu Da, who invaded the lands of Au Lac, where he deployed his troops on the Mountain of the Rusted Axe and his junks on the river.

King An Duong set out from the city at the head of his soldiers to meet the challenge. He lifted his crossbow with its magic claw and hurled three shafts at the invaders. In a trice thirty thousand Chinese bodies were scattered on the ground. The rest of the invaders stampeded in their haste to flee.

Unable to fight against a secret, magic weapon, General Trieu Da decided on a ruse in order to conquer Au Lac. As a first step in his plan, he asked for peace, and sent his own son, Trong Thuy, to the court of the king as pledge of his sincere desire for friendly relations.

The king gave Trieu Da the land situated north of the Bang Giang River. He admitted Trong Thuy to his entourage, and finally, captivated by the young man's charm and seeming integrity, gave him the hand of his only daughter, the beautiful Princess My Chau, "Sweetness of the Pearl."

✦ ✦ ✦

Trong Thuy loved his wife dearly; yet he never forgot the mission with which his father had entrusted him. And Princess My Chau returned his love with all her heart. In response to his pleas, she even showed him, unsuspectingly, the sacred, magic crossbow. Trong Thuy examined the claw with great curiosity and interest. Subsequently he had a duplicate of it made, and he secretly replaced the real claw with the imitation.

Once the magic claw was safe in his possession, Trong Thuy obtained the king's permission to return for a time to his own country. To his wife he explained: "Even the beauty of married love should not cause me to neglect my filial duties toward my parents. . . . It is now a very long time since I have prostrated myself before them." He added that he regretted very much not being able to take her along, but that the road up to the northern lands was long and rough, and that it crossed forests and mountains inhabited by wild beasts. It would not be safe for her to be along.

But, at the moment of parting, he was overcome by a deep emotion when he looked at this lovely wife, who, in her love for him and her trust in him, had unknowingly betrayed her father and her country. On her part, My Chau noted Trong Thuy's great sadness, and she sensed that it was too great for a simple leavetaking. She had a presentiment of misfortune.

She said to him: "The affection of married couples may well be imperishable, but peace between nations is, alas, often ephemeral. It may happen that the North and the South will go to war again. If, one day, I should have to leave this city hurriedly, I shall carry with me the cloak of double-brocaded goosedown and feathers which you brought to me from your country. And I shall scatter the feathers along the path by which I flee, to show you the route I have taken."

❖   ❖   ❖

Trong Thuy hastened to rejoin his father and delivered the miraculous claw to him. General Trieu Da immediately marched once more against King An Duong.

The latter was relaxing over a game of chess when the tidings of a new invasion were brought to him. He received the report with shouts of laughter. And he permitted the enemy to approach, without going out to stop them or taking any measures to defend his capital. Finally a sentry, from the heights of the ramparts, discerned the great mass of the Chinese army darkening the horizon.

The king contented himself with saying: "So, has my bold neighbor forgotten about my crossbow?" And, with that, he went back to his game of chess.

At last, with the enemy at the gates of the city, the king stood up and seized his bow. But when he loosed the first bolt, he realized that he had been betrayed. He had only time to jump on his horse, carrying his daughter behind him, and flee to the south, abandoning his capital and his kingdom.

Entering the defeated city with his father's troops, Trong Thuy searched the palace in vain for his wife. Noticing the trail of feathers which, true to her promise, she had strewn behind her, Trong Thuy threw himself in hot pursuit of the fleeing king and Princess My Chau.

In the meantime the king was crossing plains and jungles like a whirlwind, scaling hills, hurrying down declines, crossing rivers. Each time he stopped he heard the oncoming gallop of his pursuers. And he spurred his horse again, taking up his mad flight in greater haste.

My Chau cowered against her father's back, now encircling with her arms the majestic body that she had not embraced since her early childhood, now freeing herself enough to drop some feathers along the way. Even the wind whipping across her face could not altogether dry her tears. She felt herself a weak, helpless woman, battered by an immense grief.

Finally the road ended at the edge of the sea. But there was no ship in sight.

"Heaven has abandoned me!" cried the king. "Oh, Ambassador of the Limpid Waters, wherever you may be, come quickly to my aid!"

At once the golden tortoise emerged to the top of the sea and cried out in a voice so powerful that Trong Thuy heard it from afar and stopped to listen: "How can you escape an enemy that you carry behind you?"

The king turned around toward his daughter, who could only raise her tear-filled eyes to heaven, without saying anything. Quickly drawing his great sword, shaped like a flame, An Duong cut off his daughter's head. Then he followed the golden tortoise, which opened a path in the waters for him, and disappeared beneath the sea.

When Trong Thuy discovered My Chau's body, he fell from his horse and lifted it in his arms, weeping. And he bore it away for burial in the City of the Seashell.

Then, inconsolable, he wandered all day in the places that had been familiar to his wife. Finally, in a fit of despair, he threw himself into the pool of water where she had loved to bathe in the days of their happiness.

❖   ❖   ❖

And it is also said that the blood which ran from My Chau's body at the moment of her death stained red the sea at that spot, and that since that time the oysters there have produced precious pearls of a wonderful pink luster. Pearls are also said to assume a marvelous luster when washed in the pool where Trong Thuy drowned himself, where Princess My Chau used to bathe. For does her name not indeed mean Sweetness of the Pearl?

The renown of the water of this pool reached as far as China, in fact, and the emperor of China commanded that a pitcher of the water be added to the triennial tribute paid by Vietnam to China. This obligation was scrupulously fulfilled up to the Ly dynasty.

Even today a small temple can be seen on the mountain beside the sea where the princess met her tragic death. But it is especially at Co Loa Thanh, the ancient City of the Seashell, that, among other souvenirs of ancient happenings, tradition actively preserves the memory of King An Duong and My Chau. There, in the closed sanctuary of a pagoda erected for the purpose, a flame has burned before the sacred tablets of heroes in the struggle for national independence. Nearby, a sacred banyan tree, many centuries old, covers with its branches and its pendant roots the humble altar of My Chau.

In 1902 the poet Chu Manh Trinh wrote these lines about Co Loa Thanh and its legend:

Strong are marital ties, and heavy a filial debt;
Innocence, strangely exonerated, suffers even now.
The claw is without virtue, and the tortoise is absent;
Blood remains on the pearl, the oyster living in the bosom of
    the water.
A forgotten stele, an ancient tree, a thousand-year-old kingdom;
An azure sea, a blue sky, an innocent spirit. . . .
Outside the palace of An Duong Vuong, this melancholy temple;
The cry of the brook ouzel is ended; the moon becomes misty.

The Spirits of
the Hearth

ALL VIETNAMESE LEARN THE STORY of the spirits of the hearth when they are small children. This traditional legend is told them by their mothers or their amahs, and so, from the time they can remember anything, Vietnamese know that the kitchen is the sanctuary of the spirits of the hearth. For the kitchen in a Vietnamese home is a room that is much more than a place in which meals are prepared. In a way it can be called the spiritual center of the household.

And here is the story as most Vietnamese would recall it.

❖ ❖ ❖

Once upon a time, long, long ago, there lived a man named Trong Cao and his wife Thi Nhi. This couple lived serenely together, each of them devoted and faithful to his obligations. But alas, their union was never blessed with a child, and the emptiness of their hearth in this respect was especially painful to Trong Cao.

Perhaps he never intended to reveal this; nonetheless, his attitude toward his wife changed, little by little, until he became quite unjust to her. As his disposition became more uncertain, simple misunderstandings grew easily into quarrels. And finally, one sad day, when Trong Cao quite lost control of himself, he struck Thi Nhi.

Thi Nhi suffered deeply in her heart from this changed attitude of her spouse, though for a long time her love remained strong and steady. But, finally, life with Trong Cao became insupportable. One day Thi Nhi surrendered to her wounded pride and left their home. No one, she believed, could longer be happy in it. So she set out alone along the road and walked for a long time—a very long time. At last, quite overcome with fatigue, she sat down at the edge of the path. Suddenly the enormity of what she had done struck her; what would become of her

28

now that she no longer possessed a hearth? The unhappy woman sank down upon the ground and wept bitterly.

Somewhat later she noticed a man coming along the path. It was a farmer named Pham Lang, returning to his nearby hut from his rice fields, his plough over his shoulder, his buffalo ambling along ahead of him.

Night was falling. Thi Nhi got to her feet and, walking some distance behind, followed the man. When he reached his house, Pham Lang went to stable his buffalo and to put his plough away. Then he returned to the front of the house, where he saw the woman standing quietly, her eyes lowered. He looked at her silently, and then, still not speaking, he opened the door for her.

✦ ✦ ✦

Pham Lang proved very good to her, and Thi Nhi was happy again. Pham Lang never asked about her past; moreover, Thi Nhi herself seemed to have forgotten all that had preceded their meeting.

One day, while she was waiting for Pham Lang's return from the fields, Thi Nhi thought she saw him at a distance down the road. But then she realized that she had made a mistake. It was a beggar in rags who was slowly dragging himself along, seemingly at the very end of his strength. When finally he arrived in front of Pham Lang's hut, he collapsed. Running outside to help him, Thi Nhi recognized Trong Cao. A great uneasiness seized her heart.

After giving Trong Cao some rice porridge, Thi Nhi helped get him to a straw rick in a field behind the hut, and there she carefully hid him. In his great exhaustion, Trong Cao quickly fell asleep.

A bit later, Pham Lang returned home. Before going to bed, he decided to prepare in advance the ashes with which he intended to fertilize his rice fields next day. So he went outside and set a fire in the rick. By the time Thi Nhi saw this, it was already too late to prevent calamity. At the thought that her first husband might be burned to death at the hand of her second husband, and all through her own fault, she was overcome with remorse. Distracted, she threw herself into the flames.

Pham Lang saw her do this, but could not manage to stop her or to save her. In his attempt to rescue her, he himself was overcome by the flames and perished together with Thi Nhi and Trong Cao.

✦ ✦ ✦

Once they had ascended into heaven, the ill-fated trio, Trong Cao, Thi Nhi, and Pham Lang, were appointed spirits of the hearth. Their image is hung in every Vietnamese kitchen, over the hearth. From this strategic vantage point, they watch over the activities and the welfare of the entire household.

As the lunar New Year, or Tet, approaches, housewives bring home from market the ritual offerings to the spirits of the hearth, three paper hats and a lively paper carp, which they place before the spirits' shrine. On the twenty-third day of the twelfth moon, the Spirit of the Hearth (for the three spirits are often considered as having merged into one) leaves the family and, riding on the carp, ascends to heaven. (Some very modern people send him off to heaven on a paper rocket!) Arrived in heaven, by whatever means, he takes out the long scroll he has kept and, reading from it, reports to the Jade Emperor on the family's conduct during the year that is about to end. Six days later he returns in a blaze of welcoming firecrackers set off before the doorway of each household in the land. Thus do happy families greet both the return of the Spirit of the Hearth and the beginning of a new year. And when the special Tet ceremonies are over, the three paper hats and the paper carp are taken down and ceremoniously burned or thrown into a river. New ones will be provided for the spirits the next year.

It is considered very rude to the Spirit of the Hearth to sing or shout or make unnecessary noise in his presence. When servants bang the cooking pots too noisily, someone in the family is sure to hush them. Small children are taught to be quiet in the presence of the spirit, just as they are taught not to turn their backs on the ancestral altar in the family room. The Spirit of the Hearth is deeply revered as the symbol of the home, the center and focus of Vietnamese society.

The Beginning
of Good
Conversation

AMONG ALL THE LEGENDS OF Annam, this is perhaps the best known and loved, and certainly it is one of the oldest; it exists in several quite similar versions:

In the reign of the fourth king of the Hong Bang dynasty, there lived a mandarin by the name of Cao who had two sons, Tan and Lang. Although the two boys were not twins, they were as alike as two drops of water. Even their own mother confused them. Both boys were extremely handsome, they loved each other dearly, and one was seldom seen without the other.

While the brothers were still young (about seventeen, perhaps), a fire destroyed their home, burning all the family possessions and causing the deaths of both parents. Finding themselves thus alone, without resources or friends, the brothers decided to set forth together to seek work. As chance would have it, they knocked at the door of a mandarin named Lun, a very pious man who had known their father. He took the brothers into his home and developed a great affection for them, the more especially as he himself had no son, only one daughter.

Very soon Mandarin Lun conceived the notion of giving his daughter in marriage to one of the boys. Both the brothers were strongly attracted by the lovely girl. As for her, she could not choose between them, so alike they were in face and in spirit. Moreover, they vied with each other in generosity, each one wanting to yield to his brother the hand of the girl he was beginning to love.

To solve the problem, the mandarin had his daughter prepare a feast for the young men, hoping to discover a solution to the impasse in the course of the banquet. First of all, at his command, the young girl brought in two bowls of steaming rice soup, with a single pair of chopsticks, and offered them to the brothers. Without a second thought, the young-

31

er brother picked up the chopsticks and presented them, as was his duty, to the elder. The mandarin then designated Tan, the elder brother, as his son-in-law.

Because of his deep affection for his brother, and his desire to fulfill his duty as a brother, Lang quickly overcame his growing love for the girl who now became his sister-in-law.

But Tan, completely absorbed in his new happiness, neglected the ties of blood for the first time in his life. The forsaken Lang suffered deeply in this new isolation. His suffering was the greater, in fact, because of the strength and purity of his feeling for both his brother and his sister-in-law. But, bound up in their connubial bliss, the newlyweds did not notice. And so finally, unable to endure longer, Lang departed one morning from the house the three shared.

He walked far, until finally he came to a river that he could not cross. There on the bank he rested, pondering his unhappy fate; and there death overtook him. Lang was transformed in death into a rock of a white, chalky substance.

✦　✦　✦

When Tan noticed his brother's disappearance, he understood what had happened, and he reproached himself deeply for his selfishness. In remorse, he set out to search for Lang. After several days of walking, he too came to the bank of the same river. Exhausted, he sank down on the grass beside the rock and leaned against it. Soon he too was transformed, taking the shape of a tree with a very straight trunk ending in a cluster of leaves at the top, with nuts growing beneath them.

His new wife, inconsolable at her husband's absence, set forth in her turn. She succeeded in making her way to the foot of the tree, where, completely worn out, she embraced its trunk in order not to fall. Thinking of her lost husband, she wept until at last she died of grief. She was transformed into a creeping vine that twined itself around the trunk of the tree.

Alerted by a dream, the inhabitants of the district erected a pagoda to the memory of the three unfortunate lovers. On its wall they inscribed these characters: "Brothers united, husband and wife devoted."

✦　✦　✦

Later there occurred a year of exceptional drought when all other vegetation withered and died, and the tall tree and its tropical creeper alone retained their greenness in a sea of surrounding desolation. At the news of this marvel, pilgrims flocked to the pagoda from all the land.

Finally the king himself came to visit the pagoda, and the villagers

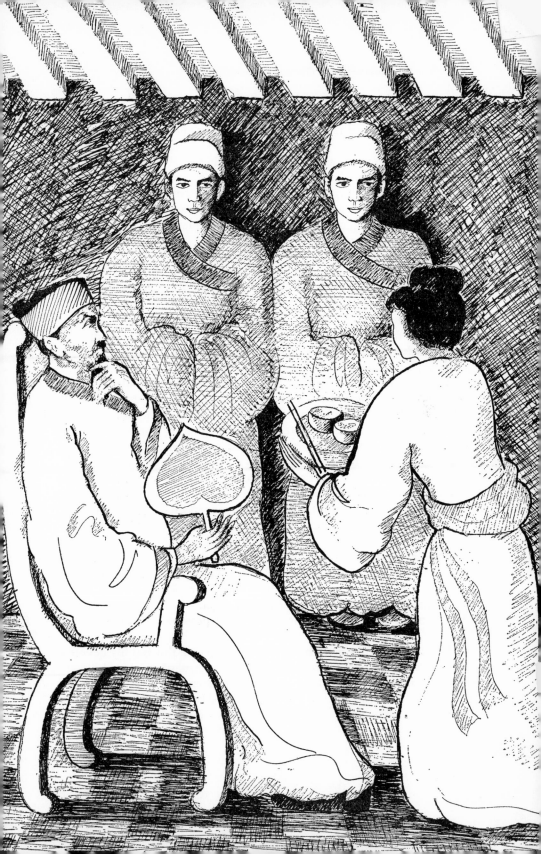

recounted to him the story of the three transformations. The king was deeply impressed and asked his counselors how he could be sure that the story was indeed true. But no one had any answers.

At last the Minister of Justice, a great and wise old man, said to the king: "Sire, when one wishes to ascertain whether two or more persons have a close relationship, one takes some of the blood of each and mixes all the blood together in a bowl. If the mixture is closely united after coagulation, the answer is positive. Perhaps we could use this same test now by crushing together leaves of the creeping vine, a nut from the tree, and a fragment of the stone."

This suggestion was followed. The stone was heated and it crumbled, becoming white and soft; the vine leaves and the nut were pulverized and mixed with the powdered stone. Thereupon the mixture took on a beautiful deep red color, as though it were but a single substance. This was proof positive of the truth of the villagers' story.

The old minister counseled the king to have the two plants distributed widely for cultivation throughout the kingdom. This was promptly done; and, given the names "areca nuts" and "betel leaves," these products of the plants became the symbols of fraternal and conjugal love. Presently people began wrapping slices of the nuts together with a bit of lime paste in the leaves of the betel vine and chewing the mixture, having found that this left a clean, invigorating taste.

The effect of this chewing can be a bit intoxicating and may seem too bitter at first. But those who develop a liking for it admire the freshness, the perfume, the marriage of sweetness with a faint bitterness. It came to be accepted that enjoying the making of the mixture and chewing it together was the best way to spark conversation; and so the serving of betel to visitors became part of Vietnamese tradition.

♦   ♦   ♦

Since the betel quid is accepted as a good conversation starter (as even an ancient proverb claims), its usage was particularly observed on the occasion of life's big events: birth, marriage, death—as well as for all religious ceremonies. The betel quid, together with a bowl of fresh water, made the purest offering to a dead person, an ancestor, or a divinity, it was thought.

But because of the association with the story of Tan and his devoted wife, it was around the ceremonies of love and marriage that the betel custom maintained its primary significance. Because conversation traditionally started with the offering of a quid of betel, the gesture became a traditional enticement on the part of a persevering suitor. The offering of betel was considered a proposal of marriage. If the girl accepted the betel, this act was considered a proclamation of betrothal. Thus a girl who did not intend to become betrothed had to learn how to refuse gracefully. In a song on the subject, a girl declares:

> This morning I was going out to gather mulberry leaves;
> I met two fishermen seated on a stone;
> Both of them stood up, speaking to me thus:
> "Where are you going so rapidly, my pretty one?"
> "Gentlemen, I am going to gather mulberry leaves."
> Both opened their sacks and offered me betel.
> "Gentlemen, my parents have carefully taught me this:
> A young lady does not accept betel from a stranger!"

In formal engagements, betel and areca, presented by the young man's parents, were distributed by the girl's family to all their relatives and friends by way of announcement. At the wedding feast the same treat was offered. And even today, if you meet an old-style wedding procession in the countryside, you will see bearers with large round trays balanced on their heads, the trays filled with bundles of areca nuts and betel leaves and covered with a cloth of red, the color of happiness.

In former days you could not enter an Annamite house without observing on the reception bed a large round lacquered box, red and encrusted with mother-of-pearl. As soon as you were seated, this box was opened. Inside, neatly arranged in compartments on a movable tray, were all the components and accessories of the betel quid: green nuts, freshly cut and juicy; dry nuts, golden at the edge and gracefully curved toward the grainy brown heart; betel leaves of clear green verging on yellow, or of dark green, heavy and firm. Such betel leaves were rolled up and laid in even layers, like cigarettes. Beside them were slices of aromatic roots, cut in rose-colored strips; and finally there was a tiny box of lime, the box often fashioned of silver and holding a fine scraper with which to make a paste of purest white. Under the tray, resting in the interior of the box, more betel leaves were stored in reserve, with some uncut nuts and a rectangular knife, wide and short, which could cut like a razor. There was a small red cloth, too, for wiping the knife.

In those days every Annamite could remember from his childhood seeing his mother teach his sisters how to prepare the betel quid properly, to raise the head of the areca nut and its green rind just so, to cut it into precisely even quarters, holding it firmly yet delicately in the tips of the fingers of the left hand; to cut the two sides of the betel leaf before rolling it, beginning at the tip; then to close it with its own edge, cut on a bevel and pricked in the middle, its inside first rubbed delicately with some lime paste.

In some families the daughters were even taught to shape the leaves in a variety of styles, perhaps like the wings of a phoenix. But even an ordinary betel quid revealed the cleverness of its maker if the completed cylinder was agreeable to the eyes in its dimensions, pleasant and firm to the touch, and with equal elasticity in all its parts.

Today the ritual and use of the betel have all but disappeared in the cities, and people no longer admire the blackened teeth that result from chewing betel. Modern young ladies may learn the arts of sewing, cooking, and pastry-making—indeed, they may even study intellectual matters—but no longer are they skilled in the disused art of arranging a well-proportioned platter of betel. In the same way, no modern young man ever offers a young lady, as pledge of his devotion, the strong branch of areca entwined with the fresh betel creeper.

Daughter of the Jade Emperor

THE JADE EMPEROR, GREAT LORD of Heaven, on one special occasion, gathered about him all the most important spirits of his court. His own daughters were summoned to serve. In the midst of the feast the youngest daughter let fall the precious gem-encrusted flagon from which she was pouring wine. The flagon broke. For this breach of etiquette, the emperor her father determined that she must be punished, even though she was the dearest to him of all his daughters. And he exiled her from his heavenly kingdom. (This is said to have occurred during the earthly period of the early Le dynasty, when the Emperor Le Dai Hanh was ruling over a peaceful Annam.)

The banished daughter of heaven was born into the world as a member of the ruling Le family. So special a princess was she that on the morning of her birth all the rosebuds in the imperial gardens burst suddenly into full bloom. Or so it is said.

The lovely young princess grew up in grace and beauty, and soon surpassed all the other women of the kingdom in these qualities. In due time her marriage to a fine and handsome young mandarin was celebrated. But alas! only three years after that happy event the lovely young wife quite suddenly died. Her husband was inconsolable. He refused to remarry.

Some years passed, and eventually came the proper time to remove the dead wife's body from its temporary to its permanent resting place. When the coffin was opened, it was found to be quite empty. The grief of the young mandarin, barely numbed in all this time, was now revived. He resigned from all his duties and retired in solitude to the province of Nghe An.

One day he was wandering there, alone in the woods, when he

reached the edge of a stream. Idly he watched the clear water rippling and splashing around the rocks, while his troubled mind followed the thread of disconnected thoughts. Suddenly a sound of leaves rustling caused him to turn around. He saw a young woman just disappearing behind a banyan tree.

The next day the mandarin returned to the same spot and waited to see if the young lady would appear again. In a few moments the wind carried to him the poignant scent of a remembered and well-loved perfume. He looked up and saw coming toward him the beloved wife whom he thought he had lost forever.

For a long moment the two were lost in a deep embrace. Finally the wife revealed for the first time to her husband the complete story of her divine origin, of her clumsiness in pouring the wine at the heavenly banquet, and of her subsequent exile to earth. She added: "When I left you, it was because I had completed my appointed time on earth. But the remembrance of our happy hours together followed me into the beyond. I could not forget them, nor you. Also, I knew of your pain and suffering and loneliness. And so I have managed to come back. . . . Unfortunately, this spring too will end; and then I fear there can be no other."

The husband was too overcome with joy at this unhoped-for return of his wife to protest the fragility of their newly discovered bliss. He decided to think no more about her words or their possible implication.

In due time the reunited couple became parents of a son, and the delight of the new father was unbounded.

One evening the couple was seated in the courtyard of their palace, sipping tea and viewing the moon. Suddenly a brief breath of wind stirred the leaves, and a faint, far-off sound of music was heard.

The young wife listened, and shivered. Then, standing up, she turned to her husband and said quietly: "The Jade Emperor is calling me back. We must part."

For a long moment her husband looked at her without saying anything. Then, at her request, he closed his eyes. When he reopened them and looked about, his wife had disappeared. There remained only her teacup to remind him she had been there but a moment past.

The young husband accepted his fate and dedicated the remainder of his life to the rearing and education of their son, who later became a great and famous mandarin.

The Silver River

ON ANY BEAUTIFUL, BRIGHT night, should you raise your eyes to the stars, you will see an immense whitish band that crosses the vault of the heavens like a scarf. This is the Silver River. Upon each of its banks lives one of the Ngau family—husband and wife—separated from each other through the will of the Emperor of Heaven. And here is their story, so sweet, so sad:

Chuc Nu, one of the most beautiful of the many daughters of the Jade Emperor, was the cleverest and the most industrious of them all. Every morning she went regularly to the banks of the Silver River, and there she pursued her daily chore of spinning and weaving all through the daylight until evening lowered its lamp. With great industry her feet worked the pedals of her loom, while her hands passed the tapering shuttle back and forth. Or again it was her spinning wheels that revolved so rapidly. She it was who made the clothing for all the Tien, the immortal beings of the court, and that is why her tasks ceaselessly mingled their rhythmic sounds with the song of the silver waves.

❖ ❖ ❖

Every day the shepherd Ngau Lang led the emperor's flocks along the edge of the river. And so, every day he observed the diligent princess at her task. Nor could he refrain from admiring the perfection of her face and the grace of her movements. Moreover, this young shepherd was handsome—so handsome that Chuc Nu could not remain indifferent to him, either.

And Ngau Lang did not dare to believe in his happiness.

When the Jade Emperor observed the interest of these two young people in each other, he resolved not to thwart them. So he consented to their marriage, insisting only that each of them continue his work after marriage.

39

But in the midst of their shared delights and new-found happiness, Ngau Lang and Chuc Nu forgot, alas, the emperor's command. The heavenly landscape offered its dreamlike promenades endlessly to young lovers, and they completely neglected their former tasks, now become totally unattractive to them.

Left to themselves, the flocks wandered straggling across the heavenly fields. No longer did the loom make its busy little song heard; spiders came to weave their silver webs on it, and on the still spinning wheels as well.

✦   ✦   ✦

The Jade Emperor proved now to be as severe as he had formerly been understanding and generous. He separated the newlyweds, forcing each to take up his former task again, but this time on opposite sides of the Silver River.

Ever since then, they both gaze up at the shining dome of the sky. Though far from each other, they think ceaselessly of each other, and of their love.

Just once each year they are permitted to meet again. The rendezvous occurs in the seventh moon, which is consequently called "the month of the Ngau."

Each time that they meet again, Ngau Lang and Chuc Nu shed tears of joy. They weep again, sadly, when the moment of parting is upon them. That is why the rains fall so abundantly in the seventh month of the year. These are the famous "Ngau rains." Moreover, if you go to the countryside at this time of the year, the peasants there will surely call to your attention the complete absence of ravens. They have flown up to heaven to form with their outstretched wings the bridge across which the husband walks to join his waiting wife for their moment of fulfillment.

✦   ✦   ✦

Other Asian countries also celebrate the legendary couple on the seventh day of the seventh moon. They say the stars Vega and Altair represent the lovers, and so they call this day the Star Festival. As Vega and Altair meet across the Milky Way, their reunion is marked with immense displays of fireworks on earth. And everyone rejoices for the temporarily reunited husband and wife.

The Butterfly in the Granary

THERE WAS ONCE A KIND FISHER-man named Quan Trien. One fine summer's day he had thrown his nets into the river and was settling back to relax a bit when he was attracted by the distant strains of beautiful, harmonious music. Charmed by the plaintive melody, he listened carefully and thought he could distinguish a flute and then a harp. Following these sounds as noiselessly as possible, he came eventually to a willow tree at whose foot he observed an old man seated, drinking wine. As the music ceased, to be heard no more, the old man politely invited Quan Trien to sit down with him and share his refreshment. So the two men drank and chatted together. After a time, Quan Trien told his companion that he must return to see to his fishing nets. But before they parted, the old man pressed his cloak upon the fisherman as a souvenir of their meeting.

Quan Trien discovered not long afterward that he had received a gift of priceless value, for this was much more than a wrap to protect against cold and rain. This was a magic cloak, with the power of making its wearer invisible.

Quan Trien was a man of very generous nature, and consequently he wanted to use his magic possession to benefit mankind, especially the poor. So, concealed by his protective cloak, he went boldly into the public granaries and took rice from them. Then he distributed this rice among the poor and the sick.

When the watchmen at the granary noticed that the supplies were dwindling each day as if by enchantment, they were puzzled, and they redoubled their vigilance. One night, thinking they heard a suspicious noise, they carried their lanterns into the granary and looked carefully about. All in vain. There seemed to be no one there.

Just then one of the watchmen uttered a sharp cry. He pointed to a butterfly fluttering about inside the vast building, directly over one of the baskets of rice. Seizing nets, the watchmen gave chase, finally trapping their prey. The butterfly turned out to be Quan Trien, who, patching a hole in his magic cloak, had used a scrap of ordinary silk in the shape of a butterfly. This was what the watchmen had seen as Quan Trien bustled about in the granary gathering up rice.

The culprit was tried, found guilty of stealing, and thrown into prison.

✦ ✦ ✦

Some time later, when the Chinese invaded the land from the north, Quan Trien obtained permission to go help fight the enemy. He formed a troop among the poor men whom he had earlier aided with his gifts of rice. They fought bravely and repulsed the enemy. In this they were immensely aided by the old man's cloak, which Quan Trien wore in battle, and which kept him invisible to the eyes of the enemy.

Because of his courage and his success in battle, Quan Trien was rewarded with the title "Marshal Defender of the Kingdom." After his death a temple was built to his memory, so that his spirit might be venerated. The feast of Quan Trien falls on the nineteenth day of the first moon.

The Search
for the
Land of Bliss

IN VIETNAM, IF A MAN SEES A really beautiful woman, he may say: "There is someone so per-fect, she must have come from the Land of Bliss!" If so, he will be re-ferring to the ancient tale of Tu Thuc, who once found this Elysium, but returned from it. This is his story:

More than five centuries ago, during the reign of King Tran Thuan Ton, there lived a mandarin named Tu Thuc who was less interested in government and administration than in music, wine, poetry, and nature. Tu Thuc was a dreamer. His book knowledge was vast, but one thing the ancient sages had never told him: the precise location of the Land of Bliss, where dwelt the Tien, the immortal beings. And this he longed to know. In fact he wanted to visit this spot, for, as a child, he had been taught that the Land of Bliss was the place discovered by the Chinese Emperor Duong Minh Hoang one autumn evening when viewing the lantern moon. Upon later returning to earth this emperor had reported that the Land of Bliss was a marvelous place, where everyone possessed eternal youth and passed the time in singing, dancing, laughing, recit-ing poetry, and feasting. All the women there were radiantly beautiful, he declared, with skin like peach bloom, and they dressed in flowing, rainbow-colored robes with sleeves like butterfly wings. They performed the graceful Nghe Thuong dance, which the emperor himself taught to the court ladies at his palace so that he could enjoy watching them while he sipped his perfumed wine in his garden under the full moon.

To live this sort of life in a place like the Land of Bliss seemed ex-tremely attractive to Tu Thuc. But he was now administrator of the district of Tien Du, where he had been posted from his native province of Thanh Hoa. One day he visited an old pagoda near his residence to view a famous peony bush in full bloom. Every year when the bush

44

flowered, its magnificent blossoms attracted a throng of pilgrims. It was now the second month of the year Binh Ti, and the flower festival was at its height. A lovely young girl of perhaps fifteen or sixteen, possessed of a quiet, serene beauty, seemed to be particularly interested in the large red flowers. Leaning close to them, she lifted a branch to get a closer look. But, suddenly, the branch snapped and broke off in her hand.

The pagoda authorities were shocked at what they considered desecration, and held the girl to insure compensation. Evening was now coming on, but no one had appeared to pay for the damage and to take the girl home. It was at this time that Tu Thuc happened in. Learning the story, he removed his brocaded outer robe and gave it in exchange for the girl's freedom. She was released and went her way.

As the story spread, everyone came to praise the mandarin for his goodness and generosity. But Tu Thuc's heart was less than ever in his official duties; thus, despite his good reputation among the people, he neglected his office and often incurred the reproaches of the senior mandarins.

Finally Tu Thuc sadly told himself: "Truly, for just a few scraps of paddy land in lieu of salary why should I stay forever chained to this circle of honors and worldly interests? I'd rather spend the rest of my days wandering the world in a slender skiff, seeking the ends of the limpid waters and the blue mountains. Thus I'd no longer be following a way of life that goes against all the secret desires of my heart."

So it came about that one day Tu Thuc untied the cords of his mandarin seal and returned it to his superiors. Then he retired to the countryside at Tong Son, whose streams and grottoes he loved to explore. His long leisure now permitted him to make many excursions, on each of which he was accompanied by a young boy—half disciple, half servant—who carried his gourd of wine, his moon lute, and a book of poems. Reaching a spot that particularly struck his fancy, Tu Thuc would sit down to drink and strum his lute. Always he sought out picturesque and unusual sites. The Pink Mountain, the Grotto of the Green Clouds, the Lai River, Nga Harbor—Tu Thuc visited them all, and celebrated their beauty in verse.

One morning, after having arisen and set out before daybreak, Tu Thuc saw, several leagues away beside the sea, five clouds of different colors and shifting shapes, which expanded before his eyes, then came together in the shape of a lotus flower. Quickly he went to the spot by boat. There he saw a magnificent mountain, rising from the sea in a place where there had never been a mountain before. He longed to climb it. Bluish mists covered the peaks, which rose to a dizzying height. Inspired by the beauty of the scene, Tu Thuc stopped and wrote a poem. His verse finished, he sat and admired the landscape for a long time. Much as he longed to climb it, the mountain seemed impossibly high. So he turned back to his boat, filled with regret, and slowly tore himself away to the waiting emptiness.

But suddenly then he saw the sides of the mountain open wide, as if inviting him to come in. Tu Thuc entered a passageway, where the darkness soon became complete. Keeping his hand on the mossy wall of the grotto, he groped his way along a narrow, twisting route. Finally he saw a light. Raising his eyes, he saw above his head some very high peaks. Clinging to the rough edges of rocks, Tu Thuc climbed until he found a wide path. When he reached the top, the atmosphere was clear and a lovely, radiant sun was shining. On all sides stood richly decorated palaces, surrounded by green and pleasant trees and pools filled with lotus blossoms. It looked like a place of pilgrimage.

Tu Thuc stood as if enchanted, under blossoms that drifted down like snow. Near his feet a peacock preened its shimmering tail. Then two young attendants dressed in blue appeared. Said one to the other: "There is the young man betrothed to this house; he has already arrived." The attendants disappeared into the principal palace to announce Tu Thuc; then they returned, bowed low before him, and said: "We entreat your lordship to enter."

Tu Thuc followed, past walls covered with brocade, doors lacquered in vermilion, and the forbidden apartments of women, through whose open doors he could see resplendent embellishments of silver and gold and above whose entrances he read such names as "Jade Heaven" and "Brightness of Jewels."

After ascending a broad staircase, Tu Thuc was led before a woman dressed in white silk, who invited him to sit in an armchair of white sandalwood.

The woman said: "Learned scholar and lover of picturesque sites, do you know what place you are now in? Do you by chance remember a meeting near a blossoming peony bush?"

Tu Thuc replied: "It's true that as a faithful lover of lakes and rivers I have wandered in many places; yet I never knew that there existed here a landscape worthy of immortals. I am but a simple man, fond of leisure; I go where my steps lead me, unconcerned about my fate. As for the peony blossoms. . . . Dare I ask you to enlighten me?"

The woman smiled: "How could you know this place indeed? You are in the sixth of the thirty-six grottoes of Mount Phi Lai, which runs through all the seas without its base ever being touched by the sun. Born of winds and rains, it is formed and then vanishes according to the whim of the winds. I am the Tien of this grotto and my name is Nguy. I know the nobility of your nature, Tu Thuc, and know too the quality of your soul. So that is why I have welcomed you here. As for the peonies . . ."

She turned toward the attendants, who understood her silent command and withdrew. A little later a young girl entered. Looking at her, Tu Thuc recognized the same young lady who had broken the peony branch at the pagoda.

The Tien spoke again: "This is my daughter, called Giang Huong, 'Vermilion Incense.' When she went down to earth to the Festival of Flowers, a misfortune befell her. It was you who came to her rescue. Never have I forgotten this priceless benefaction. Now, as payment of her debt of gratitude, I permit your two lives to be joined."

The guardians of all the grottoes were invited to the wedding ceremony, which was celebrated with music and song.

✦　✦　✦

The days and weeks fled away as fast as a weaver's shuttle. The Land of Bliss was eternal springtime, and Tu Thuc felt there was nothing more he could wish for. Then suddenly, inexplicably, he was seized with longing for the world of dust and sorrow, for the wife and children whom he had left at his native village. Often he sat awake all night near the water until the morning dew fell, the breeze died away, and the lapping waves were hushed. The tenderness of the night served only to accentuate his sadness. He felt indifferent to the beauty of the moonlight which bathed the great mountain. Sometimes the faint melody of a flute in the distance dissolved his heart and kept him saddened until dawn. And sometimes, seated in his beautiful apartments, he tried to console himself by playing on the lute the happy tunes he remembered from the world of men, but the music was somehow sad past all enduring. In his mind he tried in vain to recall the sound of the cockcrow at dawn in his native village.

One day, looking toward the south, he saw a boat on the sea. Pointing to it, he said to his wife: "That boat is sailing in the direction of my country. It's very far away—I don't know exactly where it is, but it's in that direction. . . ."

Finally he confided to Giang Huong: "My beloved knows that when

I came here I had set out only for a morning excursion, and that I have already been gone for a long time. It is difficult to lull forever the human feelings in our hearts, and you must see that I still dream too much about my native village. . . . What do you think of my desire to return sometime to my home?"

Giang Huong appeared to hesitate at the idea of a separation. But Tu Thuc pursued the thought: "It would be only a matter of days, of a month at the very most. Let me bring news about myself to my family, to my friends. Everything can be quickly done, and I shall return without delay."

Weeping, Giang Huong answered: "I dare not invoke our love to oppose my husband's desires. But the boundaries of the mortal world are narrow and limited, its days and months very brief. I fear that my husband will not find again the familiar appearance of a time that is ended. Where are the willows of the courtyard and the flowers of the garden?"

Later, Giang Huong confided her sorrow to the Grand Tien her mother, who expressed regret: "I didn't expect to see him still tied to the world of dust and sorrow. But, since he is, let him go then. . . . Why all this grief? He cannot be changed."

So, at the moment of farewell Giang Huong dried her tears and gave Tu Thuc a letter written on silk. She asked him not to open it until he had arrived at his destination. Her husband climbed into a waiting chariot provided by the Tien, and in the twinkling of an eye he was back in his village.

✦　✦　✦

Everything now appeared totally different from what he had remembered. The landscape, the houses, the people—all were unfamiliar. Only the stream descending from the mountain seemed as it had been. There was a new bridge spanning it, with strange people hurrying across it, and, at a place where Tu Thuc recalled only a marshy swamp, there was now a prosperous market place. After identifying himself, Tu Thuc made inquiry of some old men passing.

Finally one of them seemed to remember. "When I was very little," he recalled, "I heard it said that one of my ancestors bore the name you give yourself. He was chief of the Tien Du district. But he resigned his office about a hundred years ago, set off for an unknown destination, and never returned. That was toward the end of the Tran dynasty and we are now under the fourth king of the Le dynasty."

Tu Thuc then gave an account of his miraculous experience, reckoned the time, and realized that he had stayed in the Land of Bliss just one hundred days.

"I have heard that a day in the Land of Bliss is the same as a year on earth, so probably you are my forebear," said the old man. "Let me show you the old family home."

And he led Tu Thuc to a desolate spot where stood a dilapidated hut, totally beyond repair.

Feeling very alone and very sad, Tu Thuc now wanted to go back where he had come from. But the chariot had been transformed into a phoenix, which had wheeled away and disappeared in the sky.

Tu Thuc then opened the letter Giang Huong had given him and read these lines:

> In the midst of the clouds there is centered the affection
>   of the phoenix;
> Of yesterday's union this is already the end.
> Above the seas, who seeks traces of the immortals?
> For a future meeting there is no hope.

Now Tu Thuc understood that the parting from his beautiful wife might be forever.

Later, dressed in a light cloak and with a conical hat on his head, Tu Thuc climbed the Yellow Mountain in the land of Nong Cong, in the province of Thanh Hoa. From there he never returned. It is not known whether he ever succeeded in returning to the kingdom of the Tien, or if he was lost forever on the mountain.

The Dream at Nam Kha

FOR THE THIRD TIME IN A ROW the ambitious student Lu Sinh had failed in the triennial competitive examinations. Bad fortune seemed to pursue him ceaselessly, so that he had to suffer the bitterness of observing other students, less well endowed mentally than he and much less scholarly in their habits, pass the examinations and move on to success and fortune.

With great sadness in his heart, Lu Sinh left the capital to return to his native village. He traveled on foot, his light pack dangling from the end of a stick over his shoulder.

While crossing the region of Nam Kha he was surprised by a sudden downpour of rain in the mountains. He climbed into a grotto to take refuge, and there discovered an old Taoist.

The hermit had his unexpected guest sit down on the only piece of furniture in the cave, a bed of smooth stone. While continuing to watch over the cooking of a potful of millet, he informed Lu Sinh courteously about the condition of the road that lay ahead of him on his journey. Lu Sinh, in his turn, began to confide to the aged recluse the sad tale of his disappointments; he also told of his intention of starting all over again to study, of his hopes and ambitions for the future. To all this the hermit listened in silence. Then he invited Lu Sinh to stretch out on the stone bed beside the fire and take a much-needed rest before continuing his journey.

❖   ❖   ❖

Three years later, Lu Sinh met success in his struggle. He received the degree of First Scholar of the Empire. From the beginning of that day to its end, everything was gloriously and memorably arranged.

First of all, there were unforgettable formal ceremonies, marked by the proclamation of Lu Sinh's name by a herald flourishing a trumpet of shining copper before a huge crowd assembled for the occasion. Then

51

Lu Sinh, in the solemn court dress of a great mandarin, and seated nobly astride a white horse, led a procession across the capital city and on as far as his own village, where for several days festivals and merry-making went on without interruption.

Subsequently there followed for Lu Sinh the exercise of high public office; marriage to a princess, the prettiest of the emperor's daughters; then, in a few years, the births of handsome children; and eventual elevation to the rank of First Minister. It was indeed a rapid rise to the pinnacle of riches and honors, and there Lu Sinh maintained himself for fifteen years.

Then there came a sudden invasion of the country by the barbarians.

The first battles were disastrous for the empire. But then Lu Sinh was called to the supreme command, and he succeeded in repulsing the enemy. Next, he led his troops in turn in an invasion of the enemy's territory, and killed the king. However, the wild charm of the queen of that land so enthralled him that he decided to remain with her. Carried away completely by this new and irresistible passion, Lu Sinh completely forgot his wife, his own fireside, even his duty to his king and country.

In vain did the emperor summon him home. When Lu Sinh ignored the imperial command, an expedition was sent against him. Lu Sinh became an insurgent, determined to resist his ruler's troops by force; but his own lieutenants betrayed him and handed him over to justice. Despite the tears and pleadings of Lu Sinh's wife, the emperor condemned him to death.

On the night preceding his execution, Lu Sinh passed the hours recalling his entire life: his poverty-stricken childhood, his work as a student, his brilliant rise to the very pinnacle of success and power, his happiness, then the intoxicating passion that had destroyed him, his misconduct, his sudden fall. . . .

✦ ✦ ✦

Lu Sinh opened his eyes. He was in the mountain grotto, lying on the stone bed. Near him, crouching on the ground, the old recluse slowly stirred his millet porridge. Only the light sound of his spoon on the bottom of the kettle, scarcely more perceptible than the singing of the fire, disturbed the silence of the mountain. The rain had ceased.

"Young man," said the hermit, "you have had a long dream, but my porridge is not yet cooked. Just one more minute—then give me the pleasure of sharing my modest meal."

Chu Dong Tu and the Princess

THE THIRD HUNG KING HAD a daughter named Fairy Beauty. And well did she deserve this name, for never had anyone seen a princess so perfectly lovely. The princes and kings of all the neighboring countries vied for her hand. But, one after the other, all the suitors were put off. For, contrary to the ideas of most girls, ugly or pretty, the princess somehow had no desire to wed.

Years slipped past, but neither prince nor beggar took her heart. The gracious and lovely princess liked only to observe the landscape, and so each springtime, about the second or third month, she traveled with her father's permission across the beautiful kingdom of Van Lang.

The king was convinced in the depths of his heart that his daughter's decision could not be final and hence gave in to her in all her desires. In his jealous affection for her, moreover, he was not really displeased about keeping her close to him as long as possible.

❖   ❖   ❖

One fine spring morning the royal barques carrying the princess and her entourage arrived in sight of the village of Chu Xa. The area pleased the princess, and she decided to stop there. Descending to the beach, she found it very much to her liking, so she had a four-sided tent erected and screens arranged in such a way that she could enjoy sea-bathing in total privacy.

But when she was in the middle of her bath, the waves swept away some sand and revealed a man who had been concealed there.

The shock to the princess, great as it was, was nothing compared to the confusion and fright of this man. Although he remained half buried in the sand, she could see that he was young and handsome. Not daring to raise his eyes to the princess, he implored mercy and attempted to explain his unwanted presence.

53

"My name is Chu Dong Tu," he said. "My father and I fell upon great misfortune after our business was wiped out by a fire. From that time on we seemed to be pursued by a relentless fate, and finally our lot became so miserable that we had only one cotton loincloth to share between us. We had to use it in turn in order to appear in public. Later, my father became seriously ill, but before he died he told me I must bury him naked in order to keep the loincloth for myself. Of course as a dutiful and loving son, I simply could not find the heart to obey him. That fragment of cloth became his only shroud.

"Since then, I have been able to fish only at night. When daylight dawns, I stand up to my waist in water to sell my crabs and fish, or sometimes I beg alms from passing craft. Just a little while ago, when I heard gongs and bells and then saw your barques covered with oriflammes and parasols, I hid myself in this clump of reeds. But alas, you chose precisely this spot to land, leaving me only enough time to scoop a hole in the sand and bury myself in it."

Then the princess said to Chu Dong Tu: "Never have I wanted to be married. But in this situation we must bow to the decrees of fate."

Whereupon she gave the man some clothing, then led him onto her barque, where she commanded that a feast be served them. Chu Dong Tu was both entranced and disturbed. He hesitated to accept her favors, but the princess insisted: "It is the will of heaven. Why hesitate?"

So, without further delay, their marriage was celebrated there on the water.

✦   ✦   ✦

When the news of this totally unanticipated event reached the king, he was extremely annoyed. He declared: "My daughter has shown a complete lack of fitness and dignity, picking up a wretch whom she merely happened to pass. Let her never again appear before my eyes!"

Thus was the king's beloved daughter banished. No longer welcome at the palace, she established herself and her new husband in the village by the mouth of the river where they had met. Together they entered into business in order to earn their living. Their affairs prospered, the banks of the river were rapidly covered with shops, and before long the village had grown into a prosperous commercial city.

One day a merchant came from a great distance and proposed that they enter into a joint venture to seek precious goods from beyond the sea. He promised that in this way their money could be increased tenfold within a year.

The princess was very pleased by the suggestion and said to her

husband: "Heaven first brought us together, and it has clothed and nourished us up to now. This must be yet another summons from heaven, and I believe we should heed it."

So Chu Dong Tu set out with the merchant on the venture. When they reached Mount Quynh Lang, they saw a small hermitage perched at its summit. Chu Dong Tu climbed up to it in order to admire the view. At the hermitage he met a young bonze named Phat Quang, "Light of the Buddha." This monk, observing certain signs of immortality about Chu Dong Tu, expressed a desire to transmit his knowledge to him. Chu Dong Tu was inspired to accept this offer, and he abandoned his trip with the merchant.

At the end of a year of study and contemplation, Phat Quang sent his disciple back to his home. But before they parted he presented him with a staff and a hat of palm leaves. He recommended strongly that Chu Dong Tu never become separated from these possessions.

After he had returned to his home, Chu Dong Tu taught his wife the doctrine of the Buddha. When her eyes had been opened to the Truth, the princess abandoned her business and her possessions, and husband and wife set out together to seek the Way.

One evening the wandering couple came upon a deserted spot that seemed to have been abandoned forever by humankind. Even some woodcutters' huts in the distance had fallen into ruins, making the spot all the more lonely. Had some evil omen in olden days frightened all the people away? But Chu Dong Tu and his wife were under Buddha's protection, and they decided to spend a few days in meditation there. So they planted the staff in the soil, topped it with the broad palm-leaf hat, and made their temporary home beneath this insubstantial shelter.

On the third evening, suddenly a citadel arose miraculously above the staff and hat. The fortress was complete with palaces of emerald and jade, filled with inestimable treasure, such as had never been seen even in the palaces of the Hung kings. About Chu Dong Tu and his wife gathered a great crowd of courtiers, guards, and servants, all of them attentive to the couple's least desire.

The very next morning the inhabitants of the surrounding territory were seized with religious fervor, and they came to the citadel in great numbers, bearing incense sticks and flowers. They found the gates of the citadel well manned with troops and, inside, civil and military mandarins at their posts, exactly as in a well-organized kingdom.

When the king learned of these happenings, he accused his daughter and Chu Dong Tu of plotting rebellion, and sent his army against them.

As this army approached, the people of the citadel demanded permission to set out to fight it.

But the princess forbade them to do so, declaring with great sweetness: "Heaven has accomplished all this, everything. I am responsible for nothing. How would I dare to stand against my father? I must observe my filial obligations, leaving my fate in the hands of heaven. Let my father do his will. He can kill me; I shall not complain."

Night was already falling when the royal troops made camp facing the citadel across the river, on the terrain of Tu Nhien. The attack was planned for dawn of the next day. But in the middle of the night a violent storm suddenly broke, snapping branches, uprooting trees, and raising vast clouds of dust.

Suddenly, at one swoop the entire citadel was lifted into the sky, together with all its people, palaces, and animals, never to be seen again. Next day a vast lake extended on its former site.

Too late, the king recognized the power of Buddha's Way and saw how unjustly he had suspected his daughter. To make amends, and also to acquire Buddhistic merit, he had a beautiful pagoda erected to perpetuate the memory of Princess Fairy Beauty and Chu Dong Tu.

✦   ✦   ✦

In later years King Trieu Viet fought in the same region against a Chinese army sent by the Luong. Before going into battle he erected an altar and invoked the assistance of the holy couple. As a result, he succeeded in cutting off the head of the enemy general, whose troops fled in disorder back to China.

In modern times, a small market constitutes the only trace of the great commercial city created by Princess Fairy Beauty and her spouse. Of the legendary "Lake Born in One Night" there remains only the memory. But in the village of Da Hoa, in the province of Hung Yen, incense continues to burn in the pagoda consecrated to Chu Dong Tu and his princess.

The Mountain of Hope

SHORTLY BEFORE ARRIVING at Lang Son, the traveler who goes up the Delta toward the High Country will note, at the right of the old Tonkin road, a small, isolated mountain. At its summit a rock thrusts sharply upward, a tall rock that resembles the figure of a woman standing with a child in her arms. Toward evening, when the sun approaches the horizon, and the statue stands out in silhouette, this resemblance becomes especially striking. This spot is called Nui Vong Phu, the "Mountain of the Woman Awaiting Her Husband." And this is her story:

In former times, long ago, in a small village in these mountainous regions, there lived two orphans: a young man of twenty and his small sister, only seven years old. Because in all the world these two had only each other, they were very close.

One day the young man happened to consult a Chinese astrologer about the future. The astrologer said to him: "Because of the conjunction of the days and hours of your births, it seems inevitable that one day you will marry your sister. Nothing can alter the direction of your destiny."

This dreadful prediction appalled the young man. Day and night he was haunted by it. Finally, distracted by worry, he made a fearful decision.

One day he took his little sister along with him when he went deep into the forest to cut wood. Taking advantage of a moment when she had her back turned to him, he struck her a heavy blow with his hatchet. Believing she was dead, he left her lying on the ground and fled from the spot.

This act, dreadful as it was, delivered him from the fear that had obsessed him. For a long time the horror of the crime he had committed pursued him, but gradually he was able to find peace of mind. He changed his name and eventually settled down at Lang Son.

✦ ✦ ✦

A number of years passed. The brother, now grown to full manhood, married the daughter of a merchant, and she bore him a son. They were a very happy family.

Then, one day, entering the interior courtyard of their home, the husband observed his wife in the act of drying her long black hair. She was seated in the bright sunlight under a jacaranda tree with her back turned to him and did not hear him as he approached. As she slipped the comb through her sleek, damp locks, holding the hair raised high in her other hand, he saw, above the nape of her neck, a long, ugly scar.

At once he asked her its origin. She hesitated slightly; then, beginning to weep, she told him this story:

"I am not really the daughter of the man I call my father. I am his adopted daughter. As a small child I was an orphan, living with my older brother, the only relative I had. Fifteen years ago, for some reason I have never understood, he wounded me with an axe blow, and abandoned me in the forest. I would have died there, except for the fact that some robbers saved me. A little while after that, when they were on the verge of being captured, they fled suddenly from their den, leaving me behind. I was discovered there by the authorities, and a little later a merchant, who had just lost his own daughter by death, took pity on me and brought me into his home to replace her. . . .

"I don't know what became of my brother, and I have never been able to explain his strange act, which left me with this scar. We loved each other very much."

The young wife's face was bathed in tears when she had completed her story. The man mastered his own emotion with difficulty. He made her tell him the precise name of her own father, and the name of her native village.

When it was no longer possible to doubt her true identity, he managed to keep the shocking secret to himself. But he was ashamed and revolted, and felt incapable of continuing their married life. He invented a pretext for going away.

During the six months that his trip was supposed to last, his wife waited for him, patient and resigned. But long after that period of time had passed, she was still alone with her child.

Every evening she took the little boy in her arms and climbed the mountain to watch from afar for the return of the absent one. When she reached the summit, she would stand for a long time, silent, erect, her eyes fixed on the horizon.

Eventually she was changed into stone; and it is thus that she can still be seen, upright against the sky, motionless, eternally waiting. . . .

❖ ❖ ❖

This fabled mountain with its touching story has inspired many poems. Here is one of them in approximate translation:

> Day after day, month after month, year after year,
> Thinking and thinking, believing, believing, waiting and
> yet waiting. . . .
> So far away, in a thousand places, my beloved, do you feel it—
> In the sunlight, in the nighttime, through the wind, under
> the rain—
> This heart, eternal as gold, steadfast as stone?

The Gambler's Wife

TU NHI KHANH WAS THE DAUGH-
ter of Tu Dat, an administrator
living in the district of Dong
Quan. The family had come originally from Khoai Chau in the province
of Hung Yen. In due time Tu Dat arranged for the marriage of his
daughter to the son of his friend Phung Lap Ngon, a mandarin well
known and respected throughout the land for his uprightness and his
integrity.

Despite her youth at the time of her marriage, Nhi Khanh proved
herself a perfect addition to the Phung family. In addition to the fresh
beauty of her youth, she possessed a serene and tranquil nature. Always
sweet and friendly, she got on well with everyone; and everyone, in
turn, praised all her good qualities.

But Nhi Khanh's happiness as a bride was not unblemished. Her
husband, alas, did not resemble his father in character. Trong Qui loved
gambling, and this passion seemed to grow daily, until it almost consumed him. Nhi Khanh tried her best, in a quiet way, to restrain his
wastrel ways, but it was labor lost. Although she said nothing, the
young wife grieved.

After the couple had been married a short time, it happened that the
court was seeking a good governor to maintain order in the province of
Nghe An, which was infested with brigands. The mandarins who
served as advisers to the emperor, and who detested Phung Lap Ngon
because of his honesty and frankness, recommended him to their sov-
ereign for this difficult and dangerous post, and saw to it that he was
appointed. Phung decided to take his son along to assist him. In the
back of his mind he thought to get him away from his gambling cronies
for a spell.

On the eve of their departure, the old man said to his daughter-in-law: "Only because the route is long and difficult and conditions in the province extremely unstable, have we decided not to take you along with us. It is better that you wait here until peace and security are restored before joining us."

Trong Qui did not want to be separated from his young wife. But she said to him: "Surely you understand that this change of position is just a pretense of advancement. Actually, the mandarins are sending your father into the most dangerous sort of situation. Do you want to leave him by himself, a thousand leagues from here, alone from morning to night, with no one he can trust to assist him? Don't ever fail in your filial duty!"

And so Trong Qui accompanied his father to Nghe An, leaving his wife behind at Dong Quan.

✦   ✦   ✦

Not very long afterwards, Nhi Khanh lost her parents, one after the other. Piously, she attended to their final rites, took their remains to their native village, and then went to live with an aunt named Luu Thi. For some time she continued to hear from Nghe An, though at long intervals. Then all news stopped completely.

In the meantime, a military mandarin, a nephew by marriage of her aunt's, had noted Nhi Khanh's beauty and charm. He wanted very much to marry her, and he begged his aunt to arrange it. But Nhi Khanh refused. Even so, the suitor would not be discouraged, and made frequent new attempts to gain her favor.

Months passed, and as Trong Qui continued to give no sign of life, Nhi Khanh finally confided to her servant: "I've clung to life thinking of my husband and hoping to hear from him. Had he died, I should have chosen to follow him in death. I never want to be in the position of seeming to adorn myself for another man in robes received from my husband. Please, my faithful servant, I beg you, set out for Nghe An, find my husband, and bring him back to me."

The old woman obeyed. Despite the many dangers of the trip, she succeeded in reaching Nghe An, made inquiries there, and was told that Governor Phung had died and that his wastrel son had dissipated everything he had left. No one knew what had become of Trong Qui.

But, wandering one day near the market, the old woman ran into Trong Qui. She followed him to his home, an old straw hut open to the four winds, and containing as its only furnishings a narrow bamboo bed, a gambling board, and a drinking service. In a corner were penned a fighting cock and a hunting dog.

Said Trong Qui to his servant, when he had recognized her: "I have never forgotten my old home . . . but it is so far!"

The servant then told him everything that had happened and persuaded him to return without delay.

✦   ✦   ✦

The happiness of the couple upon finding each other again after such a long separation can well be imagined! But Trong Qui's nature was incorrigible and weak. It was not very long before he had again taken up gambling. He made the acquaintance of a merchant, Do Tam, who shared his pleasures. Both men concealed thoughts they would never have admitted to: Trong Qui secretly coveted Do Tam's fortune, and Do Tam coveted Nhi Khanh because of her beauty. The two men entertained each other frequently, drinking and gambling, each of them covertly on the watch for an opportunity to trick the other.

Do Tam was clever enough to let Trong Qui win often. Trong Qui boasted about this to his wife, but she reminded him that one must beware of cunning men. "They are prone to let you win one day in order to plunder you the next," she remarked.

But, in his headstrong fashion, Trong Qui would listen to nothing. He yielded neither to the advice nor the tears of his wife.

One day Do Tam brought his friends together at his house. First he served them many drinks; then, when gambling was begun, he suddenly placed a million taels on the table as stake. Trong Qui was far from possessing such a formidable sum. But, blinded by his passion, he asked to borrow in order to stay in the game. Do Tam suggested as pledge the person of Nhi Khanh, and urged Trong Qui to make the pledge in writing. Trong Qui had already drunk far too much; moreover, enticed by the remembrance of his former winnings, he held confidence in his stars. So, without further reflection, he signed the paper.

In three rounds he had lost everything.

Summoning his wife, he said to her: "I have been thoughtless and negligent, but it is now too late to regret my mistake. You must remain here in Do Tam's home until I can get money to buy you back. I won't be long about it, I promise you."

Nhi Khanh realized then that she could no longer escape the merchant's unwanted attentions. She said to Do Tam: "Who would hesitate to leave a poor environment for a richer one? You and I are both people who have longed for a happy fate, so our being together will be propitious. If you deign to cast your favor on me, I shall serve you as a servant, just as I did my husband. But first I have one request to make.

Permit me to drink a final cup of tea with Trong Qui and to say farewell to my children. Then I shall return to you."

This docility was totally contrary to what Do Tam had anticipated. Enchanted by it, he readily consented that she return home for these final rites.

Once back home, Nhi Khanh took her two children in her arms, overwhelmed them with caresses, and murmured, weeping: "My little ones, I am abandoning you only because I must. But never will it be to live with another, whatever may have been the faults of your father."

Then she killed herself.

✦   ✦   ✦

Trong Qui's grief was deep and sincere. It wrought a lasting change in him. He was finally ashamed of his past life, and he renounced gambling forever.

Unfortunately, his means of livelihood diminished day by day. Learning that one of his former friends was a mandarin at Qui Hoa, he decided to go to him to seek assistance.

Midway there, fatigue caused him to halt at the foot of an anise-seed tree, where he seated himself to rest. Suddenly he heard a voice calling to him. It seemed to come from high above the tree.

"Is it you, Trong Qui? If you remember our former ties, then wait for me at the pagoda of Trung Vuong on the tenth day of the next moon. Don't fail to be there! Never think that the world of the dead lacks ways to communicate with that of the living!"

Trong Qui recognized the voice of his dead wife, and when he raised his eyes in the direction of the voice, for an instant he thought he could see her dear form. But then he realized that it was only a black cloud there, which rapidly disappeared to the north. He thought he must have fallen prey to an illusion.

Nonetheless, on the tenth day of the following month he went to the pagoda of Trung Vuong. When he reached the pagoda, it was already late and the shadows of evening were enveloping the silent landscape in quiet melancholy. Only a few birds chirped feebly in the ancient trees.

Trong Qui walked slowly in the pagoda grounds. He felt so sad that he wanted to leave, but he decided to stay a few days and see what would happen. So he stretched out in the gallery reserved for pilgrims.

It was not until late in his third evening in the place that Trong Qui thought he heard a sound as of someone weeping softly. At first far away, the sound came nearer, and then Trong Qui thought he saw in the darkness the face of Nhi Khanh.

In truth, it was she. And she spoke to him thus: "At my death the Emperor of Heaven took pity on my unrewarded fidelity and named me to work in the service that answers mortal requests. Until now my work has kept me too busy to see you again. In fact it was in the course of carrying out a mission that I chanced to see you last month. I was on my way to bring rain to the lands of the north. Without this chance encounter, we would never have found each other again."

Trong Qui expressed his deep remorse to her and begged her to pardon him. The couple chatted together until almost dawn.

Before leaving, Nhi Khanh said to her husband: "I have had occasion to attend the audiences of the Jade Emperor, and I have heard the Tien announce that the prosperity of the house of Ho is approaching its end. During the year Binh Ti, war will break out and two hundred thousand men will perish. All those who have not cultivated the tree of virtue will risk being carried into torment. Order and peace will be reestablished by a just man of the family of Le. I beg you to rear our sons well, and to advise them, when the time comes, to follow this hero without hesitation."

Trong Qui did exactly as she suggested. He never remarried, but dedicated all his time and effort to the proper education and training of his children. When Le Thai To revolted in the region of Lam Son, the two sons of Trong Qui quickly embraced his cause and recruited partisans for it. After the advent of the great king, they attained the rank of members of the Privy Council.

Their descendants prosper even in the present day, in the district of Khoai.

The Encounter with Death

ALMOST EVERYONE HAS HEARD about Trang Tu, the old Taoist scholar who is thought to have lived in the Hung dynasty, perhaps at a time when the Chou were still ruling China. Tales about him were handed down by word of mouth from generation to generation, and all of them concerned the vast knowledge and profound wisdom of this ancient sage.

It is said of him that when death carried away his wife of many years, his relatives and friends, bearing to him the ritual offerings for a time of death, found him seated on the floor, his legs outstretched, beating a small hand drum and singing this song:

> Alas! life is like this: the flower must grow and fade.
> My wife has died and I must bury her;
> Had I died first, she would have remarried.
> Had I been the first to depart this life,
> What a great outburst of laughter!
> In my fields another worker would have toiled,
> A stranger would have ridden my horse.
> My wife would have belonged to another,
> My children would have had to submit to anger and insults.
> When I think of this, my heart suffers.
> But I look upon her body without weeping.
> Let the world mock me as insensitive and unpitying,
> For I mock the world, which nourishes vain hopes.
> If by weeping I could change the course of events,
> My tears would pour down ceaselessly for a thousand
>   autumns.

Thus sang Trang Tu in the very house where his wife lay dead. Thus sang the great sage, without the least visible sign of regret or grief.

Seeing him thus, his shocked relatives and friends said to him: "What is this? You have grown old together, you two, and have shared your years. Yet now that she is dead, you not only find no tears for her, but you even have the heart to sing and beat your drum!"

Then the great master Trang Tu arose and walked straight to the bedside of the dead woman. Pointing to her with his forefinger, he said: "Yes, there lies my wife, still and motionless! But come, do not ask me to weep for the sake of convention. Why should I weep just so that I need not be mocked and reviled for ignoring conventions by people who themselves know nothing, neither of life nor of death?"

The Crystal of Love

ONCE UPON A TIME, LONG AGO, there lived a great mandarin who had a very beautiful daughter.

Like all young ladies of her status at that time, she lived like a recluse in a high tower of her father's palace, seeing very few people. She whiled away the long hours and the still longer days by looking out her window at the broad river that flowed past the palace, far below her balcony.

From time to time, she noticed, there glided past on the calm waters the skiff of a poor and humble fisherman. While waiting for his nets to fill, he would let the skiff float free and play a melody on his flute. From afar, the maiden could not see his face at all; in fact, she could barely distinguish his movements. But the notes of his flute rose to her window, and she listened with pleasure. Although the tune was always extremely sad, the sound was pure and clear and very beautiful indeed. Listening to the flute many times, the girl came to have new dreams, and strange new feelings stirred in her heart.

But one day the fisherman did not appear on the river as usual. The young girl waited impatiently.

And she continued to wait, day after day. When she became quite convinced that the young fisherman would never come again, she fell quite ill. The best doctors in the land were summoned to attend her, but they could not discover the source of her illness. Her parents became deeply disturbed about her condition.

And then one day, as suddenly as she had fallen sick, their daughter recovered her health.

The sound of the flute had returned!

The great mandarin determined to discover what had been troubling his daughter. Eventually she told him, and when he knew the story,

her father had the fisherman brought before him. Then he led the man into his daughter's chamber.

The moment she gazed directly into the fisherman's face, the girl found her infatuation completely ended. No longer did she long to hear the sound of his voice nor to see him raise his flute once more to his lips.

But it was otherwise, alas, with the innocent fisherman. No sooner had he looked upon this beautiful girl than he fell completely in love with her.

He was seized by the love sickness called *tuong tu*. Consumed by a hopeless affection, the poor man despaired in silence, and carrying his secret locked within his heart, he soon pined away and died.

❖　❖　❖

Some years later, members of his family decided to exhume his remains and bear them to a final resting place. Inside his coffin, when they opened it, they found a sort of translucent stone, clear and shining. Thinking it some sort of pretty ornament, they fastened it to the front of their boat.

One day the mandarin, passing by the spot where their boat was anchored, noticed this stone and admired it. He arranged to purchase it, and then he took it to a turner who made it into a beautiful teacup for him.

When the cup was finished and brought to the palace, it was observed that whenever tea was poured into it, the image of a fisherman in his boat could be seen slowly moving around inside the rim.

The mandarin's daughter heard of this wonder, of course, and wanted to see it for herself. When the cup was brought to her, she poured a little tea into it; at once the image of the fisherman appeared.

Remembering, she wept.

One of her tears fell on the cup. As soon as the tear touched it, the cup dissolved and vanished from sight.

It was later thought that just one fond tear from his beloved was sufficient to calm forever the restless spirit of the fisherman. And so, with the debt of love paid, this "crystal of love" could disappear forever.

The Two Caddies of Tea

THERE HAVE BEEN MANDA-
rins and officials of honesty, integrity, and tact. Now don't smile
in disbelief! There have been, indeed, some mandarins of such exquisite delicacy, honesty, and sensitivity that the following is told of one
of them. This story is said really to have happened:

Trinh Dam Toan was a very fine mandarin, utterly honest and totally
unimpeachable, who made it a rule to refuse all gifts, no matter what
their nature or who the giver. But one day there came to his home a
man who owed Trinh a great debt of gratitude for many favors the
mandarin had extended to him in the past. The man brought with him
two porcelain caddies of tea, of the inexpensive but tastefully decorated
kind, and he timidly asked the mandarin to accept them as a small token
of gratitude and friendship.

Trinh looked at the tea caddies. Certainly this gift was modest enough
and quite in accord with ritual. But according to his fixed rule, the mandarin started to refuse.

Still, the giver, who of course would never have dared insist that his
present be accepted, had so pleading a look in his eye and so deeply
sincere an attitude that Trinh finally forfeited his principle merely in
order to give pleasure to the debtor.

When the man had departed, Trinh and his attendants noted that the
caddies seemed unusually heavy. Opening them forthwith, they discovered them to be full of gold instead of tea.

And what did the mandarin do?

He promptly resealed both caddies, summoned the donor back to his
home, and spoke to him pleasantly as follows: "I yielded to your insist-
ence and accepted your gift because I believed that we were out of tea.
But you had scarcely left the house when I discovered my mistake. We

72

do have plenty of tea, it seems. So I have sent for you to ask that you take back your gift. Nonetheless, I do want you to know that I have been deeply touched by your good intentions."

The Da-Trang Crabs

EVERY MORNING OF THE WORLD, just after dawn had fingered the sky, Da-Trang the hunter left his straw hut, mounted his horse, and rode deep into the forest with his bow and arrows. He never returned until evening, when he fetched home whatever animals he had killed. Being a skillful huntsman, he never came home empty-handed.

One day he happened to pass a pagoda near which he saw two black serpents spotted with white. At first he recoiled instinctively in fear, but, since they did him no harm, he grew quickly accustomed to their presence. Eventually, since he made a practice of following the same route each day and saw the serpents frequently, he came to understand that these were serpent-spirits. To honor them, Da-Trang formed the habit of placing an offering of game at the foot of the altar in the pagoda whenever he passed.

One day, while approaching the pagoda, Da-Trang heard a great rustling of leaves and beating of grass. Following the sounds, he arrived in time to see the two black and white serpents under attack by a yellow serpent that was much, much larger than they. Quick as a thought, Da-Trang seized his bow, drew on the attacker, and wounded him in the head, causing him to flee away. One of the two black serpents rushed after him in pursuit, but the other, seriously wounded in the encounter, soon died. Da-Trang buried it carefully behind the pagoda.

That very night a spirit summoned Da-Trang to a pile of stones outside his hut and said to him: "Today you saved me from the fangs of my enemy, and then you paid the final respects and honors to my poor wife. Here is proof of my gratitude."

Then, while Da-Trang stood watching, the spirit again assumed ser-

74

pent shape. The serpent opened wide its mouth and let fall a pearl that gleamed in the darkness of the night.

✦   ✦   ✦

Da-Trang had always heard it said that the possession of a pearl from a serpent-spirit gave the owner the ability to understand the language of animals. So, next morning, before leaving to hunt, he placed the pearl in his mouth, determined to put this adage to the test.

Scarcely had he entered the forest than he heard a voice which seemed to descend from the top of a tall tree nearby:

> "To the right, at two hundred paces, who sees a deer?
> To the right, at two hundred paces, who sees it?"

It was a raven counseling the hunter in this fashion.

Da-Trang followed the raven's advice, and when he had felled his prey, the bird cried out: "Don't forget my pay! Don't forget to pay me!"

Da-Trang surmised that just as he could understand the raven, the raven could understand him. So he put the question: "What do you want?"

The bird replied at once: "The entrails! Only the entrails!"

At once Da-Trang paid his debt to the bird.

Next day the raven was there again, and gave the hunter some more valuable information from his perch. Thus the hunter and the bird gradually formed a sort of association. And Da-Trang, grateful for the fine bags he was taking, always took care to place his feathered partner's share of the kill in a convenient spot.

But one day this share was stolen by some animal before the raven arrived to claim it. The bird thought that Da-Trang had forgotten to reward him, and he went directly to Da-Trang's home to complain. The hunter denied the accusation, of course, and protested his innocence. The partners wound up quarreling. The raven began to hurl insults at Da-Trang, who became enraged, and, in his fury, let fly a poisoned arrow.

The bird swerved and avoided being struck. But he picked up the arrow at the spot where it fell, and clutching it in his beak, he flew away at full speed, crying: "Revenge! Revenge! I'm going to get revenge!"

Several days later, Da-Trang was arrested. A poisoned arrow marked with his name had been found in the body of a drowned man. Despite his vigorous protests, Da-Trang was thrown into prison.

There the jailer soon became exceedingly amazed at his prisoner's strange behavior. He heard him laughing and talking, even though he knew the man was all alone in his cell. Naturally, the jailer thought Da-Trang had taken leave of his senses. But Da-Trang, who still carried the pearl in his mouth, was simply talking with all the little animals in his cell, begging mosquitoes and other insects and bugs not to bite him, or listening to their evaluation of the prisoners who had preceded him in this cell.

Once he surprised a conversation between two sparrows who were boasting about how they had emptied several of the royal granaries that were poorly guarded. Da-Trang immediately demanded to see the prison warden and reported this tale. At first skeptical, the warden checked, found the story to be true, and was convinced that Da-Trang had not imagined the whole thing.

A little later, some ants that were hastily transporting their eggs and supplies to higher places were questioned by Da-Trang about this rapid movement. They revealed to him that a great flood was imminent.

Alerted to this by the imprisoned huntsman, the warden hurriedly carried the prophecy to the king himself. The ruler immediately ordered that all necessary precautions be taken. Three days later the waters of the great river rose rapidly and overflowed, inundating vast areas.

❖   ❖   ❖

The king then summoned Da-Trang into his presence. From his lips, the ruler learned the whole truth, from the story of the serpents up to the vengeance of the raven. The king examined the magic pearl. Marveling, he saw in his mind innumerable projects that he could assist with it, all of them in the public interest. He hoped as well to discover for his own information more of nature's secrets and other wonders unknown to the rest of mankind. Yet he did not want to deprive Da-Trang of his pearl. So he kept him close at hand and consulted often with him, urging him to repeat all that he heard from the animal world.

Thus did Da-Trang live happily, near his king and close to animals of every species, small ones, big ones, those that walk, those that crawl, those that fly. In the beginning the king took a deep interest in these conversations and devoted a good share of his time to them. He observed that animals are not nearly so simple as one might believe and that men are wrong to slight them or disregard them or to feel too superior to them. For animals resemble humans, strangely, and each species forms a world of its own, with its own absurdities, its own cruelties, and its own miseries, quite comparable to those that affect human society.

But eventually the king grew tired of listening to animal talk, and in hope of new discoveries, he led Da-Trang in long walks by the sea. There they questioned the most varied types of fish, but there, too, really interesting conversations were rare. And the king became convinced that, like the animals of the land, the denizens of the deep spoke oftenest to say nothing, or only to do damage with their words.

On a beautiful spring morning, leaving Da-Trang to rest in the shade, the king followed with his eyes the debates of a school of dolphins. The wind wrinkled the calm surface of the sparkling sea and made the dazzling grains of golden sand twinkle.

Suddenly something roused Da-Trang from his reverie. Cupping his ear in his hand, he leaned over the water. A cuttlefish was swimming beside the royal barge and singing joyfully:

> "Cloud, white cloud
> That swims, paddling slowly
> In the blue waters of the sky. . . ."

It was so ridiculous, so funny, this cuttlefish singing this absurd song while rocking through the water in rhythm to the melody, that Da-Trang burst into laughter. As he did so, the pearl slipped from his mouth and fell into the sea.

The sorrow of the king at this turn of events was keen, but it could not touch Da-Trang's despair. They marked the spot where the mishap had occurred and summoned the best divers in the kingdom. But, as might have been anticipated, the search was quite in vain.

Though the king felt sincere regret, his sorrow did not last, for he had his own pursuits and other distractions. But Da-Trang himself remained inconsolable. Day and night, he could think of nothing but his tragic loss. No longer could he take interest in anything, and, despite the solicitude of his monarch, who remained ever mindful of the services Da-Trang had rendered him, he wept endlessly for the irreplaceable pearl.

Finally his mind went to pieces under the impact of his grief, and he conceived the irrational notion of filling up the sea in order to find his precious magic pearl again. So he assembled a whole army of workmen who scattered hundreds of barrows of sand daily on the beach. At first the king indulged him in this whim. But after a time he felt he had to stop the senseless act.

Alas! Da-Trang wasted away and died without ever fully recovering his reason. He asked to be buried in the same spot where he had attempted to fill in the ocean, his head facing toward the sea that had ravished his treasure from him.

✦   ✦   ✦

When you are at the edge of the sea, go to the beach in the early morning, at ebb tide, and you will observe numberless small heaps of sand. These are the work of "Da-Trang crabs," as they are called, which swarm about your feet and then, at the slightest alarm, dart into their holes in the sand. Using their claws, they quickly pull the sand into the hole after them. But then a single wave comes along and destroys all their work in a second. Undaunted, the crabs then start all over again to scoop and roll up more sand against the next onslaught of the waters. This goes on endlessly.

So it is said that the tireless, restless soul of Da-Trang passed into this species of crab and that, unable even in death to forget the loss of his magic pearl, he still continues in this way his vain effort to fill up the ocean.

The Vietnamese have a saying they sometimes use: "The crab Da-Trang carts sand into the eastern sea, struggling and wasting himself to no avail." This is cited each time a man is observed hurling himself into an impossible enterprise, heedless of the limitations of his strength or the frailty of the human condition. Or, more briefly still, they sometimes say: "Oh, that's the trouble and work of Da-Trang" to describe purely wasted effort—effort that a person might have spared himself by exercising a little wisdom, moderation, or thought.

At the same time they are a stubborn people and they do not mean in the slightest that one should not attempt something just because it is difficult. But still, they know that neither Da-Trang nor crabs can ever fill the sea with sand.

The Golden Tortoise

BIG HEART AND PERFECT NOBILITY had been friends from childhood. Big Heart was rich, but Perfect Nobility was poor, though content with his lot.

One day Big Heart and his wife said to Perfect Nobility: "You lack funds to do business with. Let us advance you a little capital so that you can make a start. You can pay us back whenever you want to."

Perfect Nobility reflected a long time. "I could accept," said he to himself. "These are old friends, they are sincere, they have generous spirits. But what if I shouldn't succeed in a new business enterprise? How could I possibly pay off my debt to them then?"

He consulted his wife, who shared his scruples. Together they decided to refuse the offer, resigning themselves to their poverty.

The next day, Perfect Nobility returned to the home of his friends. "I bear you our thanks, my brother and sister," said he. "But truly I cannot decide exactly what business I'd like to establish, and so I cannot take your money."

In the course of their conversation that day, Big Heart showed his friend a golden tortoise that he had just had made with all of that precious metal that he possessed. Perfect Nobility admired the craftsmanship. Then the two old friends chatted and drank together, and finally they dozed off into a nap.

While their eyes were closed, Big Heart's son entered the room. He saw the tortoise and carried it off to play with it. Later he set out for a nearby city where he went to school.

A little later the two friends awakened. Perfect Nobility then took his leave, without either of the men having noted the disappearance of the golden tortoise.

When Big Heart later remembered the tortoise and could not find it, he questioned his wife, who told him that she had not seen it or put it away. The couple was at a loss as to what to think, for they could not doubt their friend's honesty.

The next time he happened to see Perfect Nobility, Big Heart said to him: "Would you have carried away our golden tortoise in order to show it to our dear sister, your wife? Well, keep it as long as you wish."

Perfect Nobility and his wife were plunged into cruel embarrassment. "We are poor," they reasoned to each other. "If we say that we don't have the tortoise, people will certainly harbor a certain doubt. We must spare our dear friends the need of suspicious thoughts."

So they sold the few goods that they owned, and then went to call on the richest landlord of that region, Generous Opulence, who owned immense rice fields. They threw themselves at his feet and begged him to take them into his service and to give them the amount of gold necessary to make another tortoise which they could give to Big Heart.

When he had heard their story, Generous Opulence took the required amount of gold, brought it to the same goldsmith who had made the original tortoise, and thus everything was done just as Perfect Nobility and his wife had besought him. But Generous Opulence would not demand in return that the couple indenture themselves to his house.

But for their part, Perfect Nobility and his wife refused to leave, preferring to stay near their benefactor "to serve him forever with hands and feet."

✦   ✦   ✦

Some time later the son of Big Heart returned from his school, found the tortoise concealed in his room, and carried it to his parents. "Papa! Mama!" he cried out when he saw them. "You must have thought you had lost this. Fortunately it was I who had it."

The parents were totally astonished. Of the two tortoises they had now, which was really theirs? And where, then, had the second one come from?

Finally, suspecting the truth of the matter, Big Heart went in haste to the home of Perfect Nobility. He found the house empty. The neighbors informed him that his friends had sold themselves to the house of Generous Opulence.

Big Heart ran quickly there, deeply moved. He had the servants summon Perfect Nobility. When they saw each other, both men began to weep. When he had heard the story, Big Heart wanted to give the tortoise back to Generous Opulence as ransom for his friends.

But Generous Opulence said: "You have borrowed nothing from me, therefore there can be no question of returning anything. As for Perfect Nobility and his wife, I have placed them under no constraint at all to remain here. You need not ransom them, for they have never ceased to be free."

Thus the argument went round and round, with agreement seemingly impossible. Perfect Nobility and his wife considered themselves indebted to Generous Opulence and morally bound to remain with him, so they refused to go away. Generous Opulence would accept nothing, and Big Heart did not want to keep what did not belong to him.

Finally, it was necessary to turn the whole matter over to a mandarin so that justice might be determined.

But what his verdict may have been is not known.

Nguyen Ky and the Singer

WHEN HE WAS ONLY A CHILD, Nguyen Ky was noted for his extraordinary intelligence. Unfortunately, he lost his mother while he was very young. His father remarried shortly thereafter, and the second wife was extremely harsh with her stepson. She forced him to stop his education in order to care for the family's water buffalo; and from the age of fifteen, he was made to work in the fields like a man, harrowing, ploughing, harvesting. The young man endured all manner of hardships, even insults and blows.

His father did not dare to defend his son from his new wife, before whom he was weak. Eventually, tired of being badly fed, badly clothed, and badly treated, Nguyen Ky left the family home.

For a time he was obliged to beg for a living. But one day an old scholar of Dich Vong village, in the province of Ha Dong, to whose home Nguyen Ky came, was struck by the boy's fine, open face and pleasant personality. He asked him if he knew how to write. Nguyen Ky had him bring some paper and a brush, and on the spot he improvised a poem in the classical style. At once the scholar was able to appreciate the elegant calligraphy, in which grace and strength were mingled. Enchanted by the eight verses, which showed both a sound knowledge of classical tradition and, beyond that, a ripe and sensitive spirit, he then and there offered Nguyen Ky an opportunity to lodge in an annex of his house, where he would give him lessons.

Since he was extremely gifted, Nguyen Ky made rapid progress. In a few years he made up for lost time and became famous for his learning.

❖ ❖ ❖

One day a friend took Nguyen Ky to a festival honoring the guardian spirit of the village. The young scholar wore a shabby, patched gown, and when he observed himself in the midst of richly dressed young people his own age, he could not suppress a feeling of sadness. He sought a corner by himself, where he stood alone, half hidden by one of the temple columns.

Meantime, the eyes of the crowd in the temple were focused on a young singer of dazzling beauty who sang and played especially well. From her half-opened lips she seemed "to throw out precious jewels and to scatter gold." All the men were quite intoxicated by her beauty and talent, and they tried to outdo themselves in generosity, throwing silver, gold, and rolls of silk on the floor at her feet by way of appreciation.

Suddenly, in the middle of a lantern dance, the young singer turned lightly, as if hovering near the corner of the temple, and noticed Nguyen Ky leaning against his column. She was so struck by him that she became silent and stopped, her look fixed upon him. She was not able to pick up the thread of her song or dance again.

The next day, when Nguyen Ky was reading at home, the singer appeared before him.

Touching his shoulder in a friendly way, she said: "Is it possible that a man so talented as you can be abused by fortune?" She then begged him to accept some gold taels and several rolls of fine silk. Nguyen Ky refused courteously, but she insisted, leaving the gifts and withdrawing quickly, so that the student could only call out his thanks after her. He felt somewhat ashamed, but had to admit that in truth he needed this unexpected help.

Some time later the singer returned to visit him; and from then on, at fairly long intervals, she paid calls on him, busying herself about the house, mending his clothes, preparing his meals, and encouraging him at his work, quite as if she were his wife.

But there the intimacy stopped. Nguyen Ky came to respect and cherish her as a dear friend, and in both words and actions he always observed the proprieties.

One day she confided to him: "I have had many offers of marriage from wealthy, worldly men. Why, then, have I sought your friendship? I've thought about the future, and I realize that people like me often fail to look ahead. Then, when old age comes, they know only people who no longer interest them. That's why I decided that during my years of struggle and work I'd like to know a superior man, in hopes that in later years I could take refuge near him until death. Thus you must never treat me like a flower on the garden wall, or a willow along the path. In that case, I should have to go away from you forever."

Nguyen Ky understood, and from that day forward he respected the young lady even more.

✦   ✦   ✦

More than a year later, at the approach of the imperial examinations, Nguyen Ky decided to return to his father's home to see if he could secure the funds necessary to become a candidate.

At the moment of farewell, he took the singer's hand in his and said to her: "Along the miserable path of my life I have had the good fortune to meet you. My debt to you is great, and I shall remember it. Before we part, tell me how I can hope one day to attain you."

The singer responded: "Later on, if you do not forget me, it will be I who will seek you. But if fate decrees that we ought not ever to find each other again, what good would it do you to know where I am, or even the name of my native village? On my part, I dare not exact any promise from you. Let the world alone judge us, and let fate determine our future."

When Nguyen Ky reached his native village, great was the joy of his father, who had lost hope of ever again seeing his son. Even the step-mother now showed kindness and attention to her stepson, who passed the preliminary examinations with great ease, then ranked first in the triennial district examinations and won brilliant success and acclaim for his wide learning.

His proud father now determined that it was time for Nguyen Ky to be married, and he suggested to him as a bride a girl of excellent family from a nearby village. Nguyen Ky tried to avoid the alliance, and finally spoke to his father about his benefactress, affirming that he preferred death to betrayal of his hope to join his life to hers some day. But his explanation was hesitant and awkward, and his father misunderstood, remaining convinced that this attraction was merely a superficial one and that his son would quickly forget a woman of such station in life. So he declared himself flatly opposed to his son's wishes and stated that he would never receive a singer and musician under his roof.

Nguyen Ky suffered deeply. He retained his love and esteem for the girl and felt strongly that, even though no vow had been exchanged between them, he ought not to abandon her. Yet even these considerations did not cause him to forget that a man has other obligations, too, less pleasant ones, perhaps, but more imperative, and that a scholar, especially, could not escape them. And so he obeyed his father.

✦   ✦   ✦

The following year he returned to the capital to try the doctoral examinations. There the singer found him again and brought him gifts of many kinds. Noting Nguyen Ky's uneasiness, she guessed the truth.

She said: "I understand. You need not say anything. It is destiny. Each of us has his path marked out, in different worlds. . . ."

She said a final farewell to him, and left.

Nguyen Ky became a doctor of classics that year, was named a mandarin in the Imperial Cabinet, and was then appointed ambassador to China.

After his return from the north, for ten years he exercised the highest functions both in his province and in the capital. When an agitator created trouble in one district, Nguyen Ky was dispatched to pacify the area. After he had succeeded in this task, he was given the title of duke.

At that point he had attained the summit of his career. He had riches, honors, a large family—seemingly nothing more to desire. But when, among his friends, he spoke of his difficult youth, he was always overcome with emotion, and secretly he reproached himself for having abandoned the singer. Several times he sent out trusted men to seek trace of her. But the search was always in vain.

✦   ✦   ✦

One evening, in the course of a festival at the home of the Marquis Dang, Nguyen Ky noted among the musicians and singers seated below his table a woman with a lute. Her features strangely recalled a remembered face. At once he made inquiries and discovered that this woman was in truth the singer to whom he had been so obligated. Although her beauty was now somewhat clouded, her voice and her gestures had lost nothing of their charm and freshness. For his part, Nguyen Ky felt as if he were witnessing an apparition from his youth.

Speaking to his friend, Nguyen Ky learned that ten years earlier she had married a soldier, a native of Thai Nguyen. But he had been killed and she had never remarried. She had then undertaken a small business in order to support her aged mother, but a worthless brother had squandered everything she had. So she had been forced to bring her mother to the capital to try to earn there a daily bowl of rice for them both.

Keenly moved by this tale, Nguyen Ky at once invited them to come live at his home. Because of her mother, the singer accepted. Nguyen Ky placed a house at their disposal and saw to it that nothing was lacking for their comfort.

Somewhat more than a year later, the old woman died. Nguyen Ky provided her with suitable funeral rites. When these were completed, the singer came to thank her benefactor and to ask his permission to leave. Unsuccessful in persuading her to remain, Nguyen Ky begged her to accept some money from him, at least. But she refused.

At the final moment, he longed to say something to her about the past, but it was difficult. He hesitated—then, watching her leave without having been able to talk to her freely, he felt a deep melancholy in the depths of his heart, a melancholy such as he had not experienced in a long time.

And when he entered the empty pavilion where the singer and her mother had lived, there he found her final gift to him—the lute she had been playing when first he saw her, the lute she had kept through all those years of hardship.

His eyes filled with tears that were never dried.

The Tailor
and the
Mandarin

IN OLDEN DAYS, ONE PARTICULAR tailor was famous above all others in the capital city. Each article of clothing that left his hands went in perfect condition to the customer, no matter what his height, his weight, his age, or his bearing. No wonder that he was praised by one and all.

One day a prominent mandarin, wanting to order a special ceremonial robe, summoned this tailor to his residence.

The tailor appeared at the appointed time, took the mandarin's measurements, and then respectfully asked the official how long he had been in service.

"What possible connection can that have with the cut of my robe?" asked the mandarin with an amused smile.

"A very close connection indeed, my lord," responded the tailor. "Let me explain. You see, a mandarin who has just been advanced to such a position is so completely filled with a sense of his new importance that he carries his head high, his shoulders straight, and his chest bulging. A good tailor will take all this into consideration in cutting his robe, and so he will see to it that the front section is somewhat longer than the back.

"Later on, as the mandarin attains the midpoint of his career, I shorten, little by little, the length of the panels, until they become precisely the same length, front and back.

"Finally, bent under the exhaustion of long service, as well as the weight of his years, the mandarin looks forward only to rejoining his ancestors in heaven. When that time comes, his robe must be made shorter in front than behind.

"And that is why any tailor who does not know a mandarin's seniority would be quite unable to dress him properly."

Meekly, the haughty mandarin then told the tailor how long he had held official position. The tailor bowed and took his leave. Can anyone doubt that the robe he delivered a few days later fitted to perfection?

The Young Wife of Nam Xuong

IN THE REGION OF NAM XUONG there once lived a young girl by the name of Vu Thi Tiet. She was both sweet and honest, as well as extremely gracious, accomplished, and very pretty.

A young man of her village, Truong Sinh, attracted by her qualities of character as well as by her physical charms, begged his mother to seek the hand of this girl in marriage. This his mother did, carrying with her the hundred ounces of gold traditional to the ceremony.

Once married, Truong revealed himself as unusually jealous and suspicious. But Vu Thi's conduct was perfect, and nothing happened to disturb the union.

The couple had not been living together a very long time when war broke out between Annam and Champa. Truong was the descendant of a great family, but since he had never completed his studies, he was among the first called up for combat duty. His farewells to his mother and wife were touching. Weeping, they gave him a thousand instructions and wished him a quick, safe, and healthy return.

Shortly after Truong's departure, his wife gave birth to their first child, a son, to whom was given the name of Dan.

Days and months passed by. As the result of worry over her son, Truong's mother fell ill. Vu Thi spared neither care nor medication, but all in vain. The old woman soon died. Piously, Vu Thi rendered her the final burial rites and ceremonies, just as she would have done to her own mother.

❖　❖　❖

The following year the Chams were vanquished, and Truong was able to return to his home. When he reached the house he found his son, now beginning to talk. But his aged mother was no longer there,

91

and Vu Thi was absent, marketing. From his neighbors Truong learned of his mother's death, had her tomb pointed out to him, and decided to take his son in his arms and walk there. But the child refused to go and began to cry.

Truong sought to console him: "Don't cry, my son. Your father is already sad enough."

"What?" asked the child. "Are you my father, too? But you talk, and my father is always silent."

Astounded, Truong interrogated the child, who related: "Before you came here, my father used to come every evening. When my mother walked, he walked. When she sat down, he sat down. But he never carried me."

Already only too prone to jealousy, Truong was easily convinced of his wife's misconduct. As soon as she returned, he began to pour out cruel reproaches upon her.

Vu Thi wept bitterly, saying: "I was just a poor girl whom chance led to your home. I had scarcely had time to enjoy any happiness when we were separated for three years. My heart was sad, but I kept it pure. Never did I use powder or rouge to beautify myself. How could I have sacrificed my virtue, as you accuse me? I am telling you the truth. Please do not mistrust me!"

But Truong refused to believe her.

Then Vu Thi asked to know the origin of his suspicion, but he refused to tell her, giving her only vague answers and continuing to heap reproaches upon her. More than once he drove her from the house. In vain did relatives, friends, and neighbors go to the wife's defense. Truong remained deaf to their protests.

One day Vu Thi said to him: "In placing myself under your protection, I believed that I would find happiness and security, as under the shade of a strong tree. Never did I suspect that I would be buried under petty feelings, like falling leaves, or under accusations heavy as a mountain. When the vase is broken, of what use is it to climb the mountain of hope?"

So Vu Thi fasted, purified herself, and went to the edge of the River Hoang Giang. Raising her eyes to heaven, she prayed: "My humble destiny has been a thankless one, and thin has been my share of happiness. Driven from my hearth, covered with shame, I address myself to you, O gods, to you who see my misfortune and pity me. If my soul is truly pure, transform me into a pearl, My Chau, at the bottom of the water; or, if on land, to a blade of grass, Ngu Co. But if you judge that

I have failed as a wife and mother, if I have a bird's feelings and a fish's heart, let me become the food of fish and shrimp. Let the eagles and the crows dismember my body."

Her prayer finished, Vu Thi threw herself into the river.

Truong had not forgiven his wife, but now that the hereafter separated them, he wept and sought her body. In vain.

One evening when he was sitting up late beside his lamp and holding the boy in his arms, suddenly his son cried out: "Oh, look! There is Dan's father again!"

And the child pointed out Truong's shadow on the wall.

During her husband's absence, Vu Thi had amused herself and comforted the child by showing her own shadow to him, telling him that it was his father.

Too late did Truong now realize his wife's innocence.

✦ ✦ ✦

This story relates further that about this same time, and in this same village, a notable of the Phan family saw in a dream a young woman dressed in blue who begged him to save her. The very next day, a fisherman brought him an unusual tortoise he had found, which had a blue shell. Phan bought the tortoise and returned it to the river.

Later, toward the end of the reign of Khai Dai of the Ho dynasty, the Chinese invaded Annam under the pretext of placing on the throne again the descendants of the Tran. While fleeing with others from his village, Phan was shipwrecked at sea.

All his companions perished, but he found himself in a palace at the bottom of the ocean, where the queen, Linh Phi, cared for him herself, declaring that he had formerly saved her when she had been traveling in the guise of a tortoise.

In the course of a festival given in his honor, Phan thought he recognized Vu Thi, the faithful wife of Truong, among the divinities. But he dared not speak to her, being unsure. He kept looking at her stealthily.

Finally she addressed him: "We have not been separated for very long," she declared. "But you have already forgotten me?" Then she told him how, after her suicide, the river gods had taken pity upon her and had opened a pathway for her through the waters.

Phan asked her if she still thought of her village.

She replied: "My husband drove me away. He made a mistake about me. How could I ever again appear before him?"

"Forgive me," said Phan, "for reminding you that you left the weeds to cover your ancestral tombs. And can you also remain insensitive to the needs of your son, who requires your care?"

At these words, Vu Thi wept. "Perhaps I shall not always be able to hide in these depths," she said. "The horse of the Ho race whinnies in the wind which blows from the north. The bird of the land of the Viet is perched on a branch which looks to the south, toward its warm native land."

The next day Queen Linh Phi offered Phan a bag of purple silk containing ten precious pearls and had him bring it outside the waters. When he left, Vu Thi charged him to tell her husband to celebrate prayers for the deliverance of her spirit if he still remembered their former ties. She said she would later ascend to see him.

When Phan met Truong and told his story, Truong disbelieved him until he was shown an earring of Vu Thi's which she had entrusted to Phan to use as proof. Truong recognized it, and so he had an altar erected at the edge of the river, where a ceremony in his wife's memory was carried on for three days and three nights.

On the fourth day, at dawn, Vu Thi emerged in the middle of the current in a golden chariot, surrounded by other chariots, oriflammes, and parasols, which covered the whole river, appearing and disappearing by turns.

Truong called to his wife. Her response came back from far away: "I thank you, friend, but it is no longer possible for me to return to the world of men. Out of gratitude to Queen Linh Phi I have promised never to be separated from her."

As soon as she had finished speaking, everything vanished completely. And we are left with the thought that if heaven had not recognized Vu Thi's integrity, her unblemished body would have become prey for fish. Husbands, let this serve as a lesson to you!

✦ ✦ ✦

Many years later, King Le Thanh Ton passed through the province of Ha Nam and visited a pagoda that had been consecrated to Vu Thi. He was impressed when he heard the story of Vu Thi, and he improvised this verse on the spot:

> The lamp extinguished, do not go to listen to a child!
> Truong must be reproached for his great harshness.

The second line of this verse sums up the general Annamite feeling toward the Vu Thi story. But the poet Nguyen Cong Tru saw the paradox in her action and composed a song on the subject, of which these lines are a fragment:

> Her heart was pure, but her motive was wrong.
> She was true to her husband; why did she fail her son?
> It is not suitable to accuse the man of harshness
> Since, in darkness, each of us has only his own lamp for
>   illumination.

The Saint of Children

LONG, LONG AGO, IN THIS SERENE land, there lived a young girl named Thi Kinh. So celebrated for her beauty was she that the richest and most brilliant suitors vied for her attention. But Thi Kinh's humility and her devotion to the Path of the Buddha were so great that she refused everyone of position or power, choosing for her husband a man without either fortune or great personal attractiveness.

Life was often difficult in the new household, but the young wife accomplished joyfully even the hardest and most menial tasks, discovering her happiness in faithful devotion to her husband and unswerving affection for him.

One afternoon she paused in her household chores to gaze fondly at her husband as he lay napping. Noticing that a hair of his beard was growing the wrong way on his chin, she decided to remove it. Taking a very sharp knife in her hand, she approached the sleeping figure. Her husband woke up with a start, took fright, and moved suddenly in his agitation, so that his face was slightly cut. Convinced that his wife must be making an attempt on his life, he cried out for help.

Surprised at first, then dismayed and deeply grieved, poor Thi Kinh did not know what to say to her angry husband and the hostile neighbors who had come crowding in. In her submission and sorrow, she kept silent. This air of resignation was interpreted as admission of guilt, and Thi Kinh's husband drove her from the house.

No one would take any pity on her. Her former friends turned away at her approach. Her former suitors, as well as their wives, who could not forgive Thi Kinh her beauty, vied with each other to insult her. Her own family disowned her.

Abandoned by everyone, despised, lacking anyone to turn to, Thi

Kinh chose the path of forgetfulness and renunciation. Disguising herself as a man, she entered a pagoda and asked for admission into the community of Buddhist monks there.

But even now a life of peace was not granted Thi Kinh. For among the faithful laity who frequented the pagoda, one young girl was not long in noticing the beauty of Thi Kinh's face, despite the humbleness of her religious robe. This impressionable girl sought vainly to attract the new monk's attention. Failing in this, she accosted Thi Kinh one day and spoke to her shamelessly. Realizing the error the girl was making, Thi Kinh stopped her, begging her to respect her religious vows, but not revealing her sex.

Rebuffed in this fashion, the young girl decided from spite to wed a man who was courting her. Some time later she became a mother. When the child was born, the girl placed the infant in a basket and left him at the pagoda with a note declaring the new monk—Thi Kinh—to be the child's father.

When the basket was brought in, the superior was surrounded by all the monks in the community. As he read the note accompanying the infant, the baby began to cry. Thi Kinh leaned over the child and, with the instinctive reaction of a woman, lifted him to soothe him. This natural gesture was misconstrued. In the eyes of everyone present, it confirmed the accusation. Thi Kinh was driven from the community.

At first the poor woman was tempted to put an end to her life. But she took such pity on the abandoned child that she resigned herself to her tragic lot. To get food for them both, Thi Kinh now became a beggar, and thus she lived for some years, wandering along the roads with the child in her arms and her begging bowl in her hands.

Finally when she felt her strength flagging, she dragged herself back to the pagoda and knocked for the last time at the door of the Buddha. In a few words she recounted her misfortunes to the abbot, beseeching that no harm be done to those who had caused it. She begged him to pardon her use of a disguise. She confessed that from the time when she had first known happiness with her husband, she had been too attached to the earth and to earthly pleasures, to material things, and to herself. Then, confiding to the abbot the child that she had accepted as her son, Thi Kinh died peacefully.

✦ ✦ ✦

When the sad story of Thi Kinh was brought to his attention, the emperor was struck with admiration for her purity and self-abnegation. By imperial decree he caused her to be raised to the rank of divinity, with the title Quan Am Tong Tu, "Merciful Protector of Children." Her cult spread quickly all through Asia.

Even today Thi Kinh can be seen, amid the oblivion in which the old Annamite pagodas sleep. Under roof beams blackened by ancient incense, among crumbling statues of worm-eaten wood which peer out into the semi-darkness, there you will see the saint seated, the child in her arms, the tenderness of a changeless smile on her gentle, serene face.

The
Portrait
of the Tien

ONCE LONG AGO IN ANNAM THERE lived a student named Tu Uyen. The young man was devoted to the pursuit of knowledge, spending most of his time in solitude, practicing his calligraphy and writing verses.

But one day he went out to attend a festival at a nearby pagoda. He was returning slowly homeward, admiring the countryside and the beauty of the sky, when suddenly he saw fall in front of him a sheet of paper bearing some characters. He leaned down to read them. They were verses of invitation to attend one of the poetry contests that were then traditional.

Raising his eyes again, he noticed, standing at the foot of a tree, a young girl of surpassing, ethereal beauty. She smiled at him; he composed a reply to the written verse in a verse of his own; and the couple began to walk along together, composing alternate lines of verse which they recited in an artistic competition. But after a short time, the lovely young lady suddenly disappeared. Tu Uyen then understood that he had met a Tien or heavenly spirit. For a long time he stood in reverie, unable to make up his mind to leave the spot.

From that day forward, he never ceased thinking of that amazing encounter. "He neglected to sleep during the five watches of the night; he forgot to eat during the six divisions of the day." In a word, Tu Uyen was seized by a languor of love, the sickness for which it is impossible to find a cure.

But he remembered the famous oracles of the Pagoda of the White Charger, sacred to the genie of the River To Lich. One evening he betook himself there, prostrated himself, and prayed. That night he slept in the pagoda.

An old man with white hair floating in the breeze, leaning on a stick of knotty bamboo, appeared in a dream and said to him: "Tomorrow when you awaken, go to the Eastern Bridge. There you will find what you are seeking."

Tu Uyen awakened early the next morning and joyfully ran to the Eastern Bridge. But no one was there. He waited for a long time, feeling an increasing dismay. Then, as he was on the point of leaving, he noticed an old man selling scroll paintings. Tu Uyen looked at the paintings and to his surprise saw one that represented perfectly the young lady he had seen so briefly, had met and lost.

Tu Uyen bought the portrait of the Tien and hung it in his room. There he talked to it as if it were a living person, touched it, and endowed it with the attributes of the girl herself. In this way he was able to dispel his incurable sadness and return to work. At each meal he placed on the table two bowls with matching pairs of chopsticks, and never did he serve himself until he had first served the young lady of the portrait, exactly as a husband would serve his wife.

One day, in response to his invitation to dine, he thought he saw the face in the picture smile. The next day when he returned from the home of his teacher, the meal was already prepared! When he tasted it, everything seemed unusually exquisite. The following day, Tu Uyen made a pretext of departing to his teacher's home as usual, but then he suddenly returned. He surprised the young Tien, who had descended from the portrait, in the act of arranging her hair.

Without raising her eyes, she said: "My name is Giang Kieu, and I live in the palace of the Tien. In your family there is a great accumulated fund of predestined happiness, which permitted our first encounter. Then, when the queen of the Tien saw that you couldn't forget me, she permitted me to come down to earth to keep your house."

In order to keep her close to him this way, Tu Uyen took the portrait from the wall and tore it to pieces.

Giang Kieu then pulled a pin from her hair and caused a palace to appear, with sumptuous furniture and a crowd of servants. They had a great celebration in the palace, and many Tien descended to attend their wedding.

The life of Tu Uyen and Giang Kieu was idyllic, totally without strife or discord. They had one son, who succeeded brilliantly in his studies.

When their son was approaching manhood, Giang Kieu said to her husband: "In this lower world, a human life does not last one hundred years. But your name is inscribed in the Book of Immortals. It is time

now for me to depart to the heavenly regions. To prevent separation, let us now ascend together to the kingdom in the skies."

Whereupon she gave an amulet to Tu Uyen. Then two cranes descended from the skies to bear them away. Before flying off on the cranes, Tu Uyen and Giang Kieu turned to their son and said: "All our earthly possessions are now yours. Continue your studies and await us here. When it is time for you to depart the earth, we shall return together for you."

Later on, the villagers erected a pagoda on the spot where Tu Uyen's house had stood, so that a cult was created in his memory. The Tu Uyen Pagoda was located in Hanoi near the Eastern Bridge, which no longer exists, but which was situated, they say, between Sugar Street and Copper Street. And the River To Lich no longer flows in those parts, as it used to do.

At the site of the South Gate, near the spot where the original meeting between Tu Uyen and the Tien took place, Neyret Place extends today. But now the area holds shops, bicycle shelters, and police boxes. It seems unlikely that Tien come down there now to make verses.

The Cook's Big Fish

TU SAN OF THE LAND OF TRINH prided himself upon being a disciple of Confucius and following the wisdom and teachings of both Confucius and Mencius. He was renowned for his great knowledge.

One day his cook, a weak, friendly fellow, with a great love for gambling, was lured into a game of chance by some comrades and, running into a streak of bad luck, lost all the money entrusted to him for the day's marketing.

Fearful of being reprimanded severely when he returned home empty-handed, the cook dreamed up the following tall tale, which he related to Tu San:

"This morning when I got to the market I noticed a large fish—very plump, very fresh, truly a superb specimen in every way! Just out of curiosity, I asked the price. To my astonishment, they wanted only one tael for it. Why, a fish like that was easily worth two or three! It looked to me like a big bargain, so, seeing a chance to make a delicious dish for my master, I bought it with the money you had given me for the day's shopping.

"I started directly home, carrying the fish wrapped in fresh leaves at the end of a piece of string. Halfway home I noticed that the fish seemed to have become stiff. Perhaps he had died, I thought. I remembered the old saying: 'A fish out of water is a dead fish!' By good luck, I was just then passing a small pond, so I hurriedly plunged the fish into the water in hopes of reviving it in its natural element.

"But after a few moments in the water, it appeared still to be lifeless. So I pulled the string out and held the fish between my hands. Soon he moved a bit, gaped, and then, in one swift movement, slid from my fingers. I stretched out my arms to recapture him, but with a flip of his

104

tail he moved off through the water, out of sight. . . . I confess, I have behaved very stupidly."

When the cook had finished his tale, Tu San clapped his hands together and said admiringly: "Why, how fine, how perfect!" (Was he admiring the cleverness of the fish's escape?)

The cook withdrew from his master's presence, secretly laughing up his sleeve at the man's incredible gullibility. The cook sought out his friends and boasted: "Who in the world can possibly pretend to believe that my master has a great intellect? I took the marketing money and lost it all in a game of chance. Then I made up a story to cover up, and he swallowed the whole thing without questioning it for a moment. No, certainly my master has no great intellect!"

Indeed, as Mencius so wisely said: "A plausible lie can fool even a superior being." (Or was it the cleverness of his cook's story that made Tu San clap his hands?)

It doesn't really matter. For, said Confucius himself, "To those who lack wisdom, the truly wise man often appears to be a fool."

Brothers and Friends

A FATHER DIED, LEAVING TWO sons but no will. As a result, the elder brother, Kim, seized the entire heritage, turning over to his younger brother De only a straw hut and a small piece of dry, arid land, on which De could barely eke out a living for himself alone.

Although he thus proved himself hard and unfeeling to his younger brother, Kim was just the opposite to his numerous friends. Among them he was unfailingly obliging and generous. He received them with magnificent hospitality, helped them in every circumstance. Should one of them find himself in some sort of trouble, no matter what the reason, he knew he had only to knock on Kim's door to be sure of assistance. Kim would spring to their aid even before they had time to express their wishes.

His wife, who was good-hearted and just, was completely astonished at this conduct. She remonstrated with him time and again about the severity of his attitude toward his own brother as contrasted with his willingness to do anything for his friends. But to all her chiding Kim regularly responded that De was certainly big enough now to get on alone in the world, whereas his friends were quite remarkable and extremely devoted men who deserved every ounce of friendship he could extend them.

Such foolish explanations totally failed to satisfy his wife. She continued to repeat: "Brothers are like parts of the same body, whereas friends, however likable, often prove to be either selfish or else parasitic flatterers. You just cannot count on them in critical situations."

De was well aware of his sister-in-law's kind sentiments toward himself, and he often came to call at his brother's home, not confining his visits to those formal anniversaries and festivals when his presence was demanded by convention. More, he never permitted the least shadow of resentment against Kim to show in his manner, nor the least trace of bitterness, for he did not want to sadden his sister-in-law. She herself never dared to suggest helping him, nor to defend him openly, for fear of wounding his pride. At the same time she never totally despaired of guiding her husband back to the right path of conduct.

One evening when he returned home, Kim found his wife in tears. She said to him: "Just a little while ago a beggar came to the door asking alms. I was busy in the kitchen, so I called out to him to wait. He observed that the house was empty except for me, and that I was in the kitchen, so he crept noiselessly into the front part of the house and was trying to steal some things when I surprised him. In my anger, I struck at him too violently. He fell, striking his head against the edge of the bed. The blow killed him! I was stunned and didn't know what to do. Finally I wrapped his body in a mat and dragged it into the garden."

Kim was even more upset than his wife at this revelation. He had no idea what to do next.

His wife, still weeping, reminded him: "We are not on the best of terms with the mandarin. Even though I didn't intend to kill the beggar, who can say what judgment the mandarin may hand down? We'll be involved in a scandal and ruined!"

At this the husband fell into even greater panic. Then it was that his wife insinuated to him: "The beggar is dead. Our punishment would not bring him back to life. . . . If we could just bury him secretly in the woods, no one would ever need to know anything about it. Get some of your most dependable friends to help you, since you can't manage it alone. Your friends all owe you so much, not one of them surely will refuse to give you a proof of his gratitude and devotion when you need it so desperately."

Reassured and full of hope, Kim went then to knock at the gate of the friend who lived nearest to him. This friend opened up to him with a big smile, but the smile gradually faded in the face of Kim's extreme seriousness. Then, after Kim explained what had brought him, the friend's attitude changed. He expressed his regrets: he was very old, very weak, he would never be able to carry a heavy load, he would only hold Kim back. . . . Kim would be better advised to ask someone else who would be stronger. . . .

Kim ran to the home of another friend. Here he was received with the greatest warmth and invited in for a cup of tea. The host even suggested that he go seek partners for a card game. But Kim began to explain hurriedly the purpose of his visit. The friend promptly discovered a serious handicap . . . his mother-in-law had been seized with an unfortunate illness, and he was overdue at her home. . . .

The third friend to whom Kim had recourse was immediately struck by his frantic appearance. Before Kim could open his mouth to speak, this friend said to him: "Something is bothering you. Tell me your problem. Everything must be shared between friends. Perhaps I can help you."

Kim felt that now at last he was saved. Overflowing with joy and gratitude, Kim unburdened himself to this friend. But, alas! this one too found an imperative reason that prevented his going along to help Kim. But that did not hinder him from sharing Kim's concerns, from pitying him with all his heart, from wishing that he could be of assistance, though under the present circumstances. . . .

Now Kim felt truly that he was lost. Each of the friends to whom he had appealed had in effect given the same no for an answer, and doubtless they would already have warned his other friends, who would now be preparing their excuses. There was no reason to seek or expect further help. Filled with despair by such thoughts, he returned home.

There his wife revived his courage, reminding him of what she had always told him. She urged him to knock at last at the door of a humble home where he would not meet with refusal. "You must go now to De's house. Hurry!"

The poor man no longer possessed will power. He hesitated for a moment, but then dragged himself to the straw hut of his younger brother.

De was very surprised to see Kim, especially as it was quite late. He cried out: "How pale you are, brother! What is the trouble? Is my sister-in-law sick?"

When he learned what had occurred, De did not hesitate an instant. He followed his elder brother back to his house.

"My sister is right," he said. "Two men are needed for this task."

When everything was finished, it was long past midnight, and Kim was at the end of his strength.

Early the next morning a message was received summoning Kim and his wife immediately to the home of the mandarin. Alarmed, they went without delay, arriving to find already gathered there all those friends of whom Kim, in his confusion and need, had sought assistance.

In their presence, the mandarin spoke severely to the couple: "You have killed a beggar and secretly buried him. You even had the effron-

tery to try to drag good, honest citizens into your plot. Fortunately they obeyed only the voice of their conscience, and have revealed your guilt."

De had followed his brother and sister-in-law to the mandarin's home. From all that was said, the two brothers realized that their accusers had probably followed them into the woods the night before.

"Don't try to deny your guilt," said the mandarin, "for we know exactly where you have concealed the body and we are going to go there right now and exhume it."

So this was done. (Pray note that Justice is not always slow.) But imagine the general astonishment when, once the matting was unrolled, the body of a large white dog was revealed!

The mandarin frowned, and the accusers were extremely discomfited. As for Kim and De, they simply did not know what to think, but whatever lay behind the matter, they were certainly relieved at this unexpected outcome.

Then Kim's wife asked permission to explain everything. For a long time, she declared, she had reflected on a method to open her husband's eyes to people in general, and to his friends in particular. She wanted him especially to recognize that fraternal ties are deep and sacred. The unexpected death of her dog, which had occurred the day before during Kim's absence, seemed finally to supply her with the opportunity she had been looking for. So she had thought up the situation which had brought them all together at this spot.

At the mandarin's order, the faithless friends each received fifty strokes of a bamboo cane. Somehow the mandarin was so annoyed at having been tricked into digging up a dog that he quite forgot he had been praising these men only a short time before, and instead he blamed them for his embarrassing situation. (Pray note also that Justice is not always logical.)

As for Kim, the lesson he learned that difficult night and day made a tremendous impression upon him. Never thereafter did he forget the torrent of emotions that had shaken him during that awful time, and from that day forth there was no more loving elder brother in all the land than Kim.

And as for the wife and younger brother—well, you are left to imagine their new-found happiness in having such a fine man for husband and brother.

You Are Right!

MAJESTICALLY ENTHRONED ON a dais in the great hall of his ya-men, a mandarin was listening to official complaints and dispensing justice.

Behind the magistrate hung a magnificent scroll of calligraphy, and articles for his use were carefully arranged around him. At some little distance in front of him there was a large teakwood table holding an inkstone, brushes, provincial registers, and long rolls of rice paper. Nearer at hand were his teapot and teacup and his long-stemmed water pipe, its bowl elegantly encrusted with mother-of-pearl, above which rose the slim cylinder of the pipe's long bamboo tube.

The mandarin pointed with his forefinger to a peasant standing beyond the teakwood table. "You there!" commanded this father-and-mother-of-the-people, "state your complaint."

The peasant, dressed for the occasion in garments only slightly less ragged than usual, was a tall, able-bodied man. He scratched his head conscientiously, disarranging his badly rolled turban in the process. Then, with many pauses and repetitions and stammerings, the poor fellow gave a long, labored account of his griefs.

The mandarin seemed to listen with careful attention. From time to time he waggled his head up and down judiciously, as though agreeing with what he was hearing.

Finally, after a pause considerably longer than any of the others, the peasant appeared to have ended his tale.

The mandarin cried out: "Pipe!"

An attendant immediately rushed forward, tamped a pinch of tobacco into the little bowl, lighted it, and, flexing the bamboo stem, handed the pipe to the mandarin. That worthy gentleman closed his lips over the silver mouthpiece and sucked in his cheeks, closing his eyes the while as though deep in thought. The pipe hummed a moment with a

111

joyous bubbling sound, and then was silent again. Two wreaths of smoke emerged from the patrician nostrils, and for an instant a pale-blue cloud veiled the half-closed eyes. Everyone was respectfully silent as the mandarin pondered.

Suddenly the mandarin's voice broke the stillness: "You are right!"

At this point, the mandarin turned around toward the defendant in the case, who was standing at his left, and demanded: "You there, what do you have to reply to all this?"

That poor devil scratched his head as scrupulously as had his adversary, and then he spoke in reply for just as long a time, and in almost as halting a manner.

The mandarin heard him out with the same patience, dignity, and rapt attention. At the end, when the story was finished, the mandarin commanded a second pipe, and the same ceremonial lighting of the tobacco was conducted a second time.

Finally, with everyone's attention centered upon him, the mandarin made known his considered verdict: "You are right, too!"

At just this moment the mandarin's wife—the "honorable great lady"—who had been listening to everything from the privacy of a neighboring room, swept into the hall of justice, crying out: "What? What method of rendering justice is this? How can you find for both the plaintiff and the defendant at the same time?"

Without stopping to reflect, the mandarin faced his wife and spoke in a voice of gentle humility: "You are quite right, my dear. I was wrong to approve both sides."

✦   ✦   ✦

It is from this tale that the Vietnamese get a common expression: *Ong Ba Phai*. This can be translated as "Mr. Three Yesses" or "Mr. Three Times: That's Right" or even as "Mr. Three Times: You are Right." The mandarin's magnificent pipe is said to be still in existence, but who knows how the two peasants ever settled their dispute?

The Mosquitoes

IN VIETNAM MOSQUITOES ARE AL-
ways bothersome and, during the
rainy season, often quite unbear-
able. Everyone hates them—but those who know this story concerning
them are few. Perhaps only a score or so of people in all the land realize
why these miserable insects hum ceaselessly in our ears while constantly
seeking an opportunity to steal some of our precious blood. This is the
reason:

Ngoc Tam, a humble rice farmer, had married Nhan Diep. Both husband and wife were young and of good breeding, and they seemed well
mated and destined for the joys of a simple but industrious life. Ngoc
Tam busied himself ceaselessly with the care of his rice fields and of one
small field of mulberry trees. Nhan Diep raised silkworms.

But this Nhan Diep, alas, was inclined to be lazy and coquettish.
While she tended her silkworms, she dreamed of a life given over to
luxury and pleasures. All these dreams and desires she carefully concealed from her husband, for his tastes and ambitions were quite different. Because his nature was stolid and affectionate, he was neither de-
manding nor questioning, and so he continued to believe that his wife
was content with her lot and happy to help him. So he struggled all the
harder to better their mutual fortune.

Then, without warning, Nhan Diep died. Ngoc Tam's shock was
great, his grief inconsolable. He refused to be separated from his wife's
body, refused to have it buried. Instead, he sold all his belongings,
bought a sampan, placed his wife's coffin tenderly on it, and with it
drifted out on the stream.

One morning, after aimless wandering on the waters, Ngoc Tam
found himself at the foot of a verdant, flower-carpeted mountain, from
whose sides drifted a sweet perfume. Stepping onto the land, he found

himself walking on a carpet of thousands of rare wildflowers, beneath trees loaded with magnificent fruits. Enchanted, he continued to walk up the mountainside, not realizing the height to which he had ascended until he noted that he was beginning to feel quite giddy.

Suddenly he observed, standing facing him on the path, an old man leaning on an oddly shaped bamboo staff. His hair was white as cotton; his wrinkled face, a bit sunburned, shone with a gleam of youth and health; and his eyes sparkled like those of an adolescent from under white eyebrows. Looking into those eyes, Ngoc Tam recognized the genie of medicine, Tien Thai, who travels across the world on his mountain to teach his science to men and cure their illnesses. Ngoc Tam threw himself at this spirit's feet.

The genie spoke to him: "Because I know about you and your virtues, Ngoc Tam, I decided to stop my mountain along your way. If you wish to become one of my disciples, I shall be pleased to accept you into their company."

Ngoc Tam thanked the spirit humbly, but said that he was finding it impossible to live without his well-loved wife. He added that he could not conceive of a life other than that which he had led with her, and he begged the spirit, if it so lay within his power to accomplish, to bring her back to life again.

The genie gazed at him with kindness mingled with pity. He said: "Why do you permit yourself to become trapped in this world of affliction, where joys are rare and serve only as snares? What folly, to entrust your precious self and your happiness to another weak, inconstant being! Well, all right, so be it. I am willing to grant you your wish; but I shall have to hope that you won't regret it later on."

At his command, then, Ngoc Tam opened the coffin, cut the end of his finger, and permitted three drops of blood to fall on the body of Nhan Diep. She opened her eyes slowly, as if awakening from a deep sleep. Her strength returned quickly.

"Don't forget your obligations to your husband," said the genie to her. "Think of the devotion that you owe your husband. . . . May you both be happy!"

✦   ✦   ✦

During the return trip Ngoc Tam rowed day and night, impelled by a strong urge to get back to his own hearth. One evening, en route, he entered a harbor to seek provisions. During his absence from his sampan, a large boat pulled up alongside it, and the owner, a rich merchant, noticed Nhan Diep and was struck by her beauty. He entered into con-

versation with her and invited her to join him in a cup of tea, but as soon as she was in his boat, he set the sails and departed.

At the end of a long month of searching, Ngoc Tam found his wife again. But by that time the inconstant woman had grown very accustomed to her new life, which suited her admirably. In response to her husband's questions, she admitted this quite frankly and without evasion. For the very first time her husband saw her in her true light. Then and there he became completely cured of his love for her. No longer did he regret her or pine for her.

"You are completely free," he told her. "Only give back to me the three drops of blood that I shed to bring you back to the land of the living. I don't want you to retain in yourself the least part of me."

Happy to win her freedom so cheaply, Nhan Diep hastened to seize a knife and to cut the end of her finger. But scarcely had the blood begun to flow than she grew frightfully pale and sank to the ground. People nearby rushed to her aid. But she was dead.

✦　　✦　　✦

Even after she had thus died a second time, the inconsiderate and fickle wife could not resign herself to quitting the world and its pleasures forever.

Instead, she returned to the earth in the form of a swarm of small insects. The insects followed Ngoc Tam incessantly, seeking to steal from him the three drops of blood that, they foolishly believed, would restore the dead woman to human life again. They pestered poor Ngoc Tam endlessly, and their pleas that he forgive his dead wife for her past conduct, their protestations of regret and repentance—these were the angry humming and buzzing that he heard about his ears.

Presently the insects were given the name "mosquitoes." Most unfortunately for the human race, even though the blood they stole from poor Ngoc Tam was of no avail, the breed multiplied and buzzes around our ears to this day.

The Child of Death

JUST A MONTH BEFORE SHE WAS TO have become a mother, a young peasant woman was carried away by a sudden illness to the Land of the Dead.

A few moments before her death, the young wife had looked steadily at her husband, with a directness that was contrary to her customary reserve. And, even though there were friends in the room with them, he could not help leaning close to see what she wanted.

He heard her murmur: "The baby . . . our child . . ." And then she was silenced by death.

The bereaved husband uttered a cry of deep anguish, became terribly distressed, and cried out, sobbing.

Such an unusual display of violent grief astonished his friends. In this land of Vietnam, you see, people are accustomed to misfortunes, especially when they are not rich, and they usually accept whatever comes their way with stoic resignation. And everyone must work hard; there is little time left over for complaining and bemoaning one's fate.

Even this poor peasant soon had to dry his tears. And the day after his wife's burial he was again in his fields, behind his water buffalo and his plow.

A few days later an old woman of the neighborhood who was almost blind and who sold betel and other small provisions at a straw hut near a culvert in an open field was approached by a young woman who somehow seemed vaguely familiar. The woman came to the hut and bought a few coins' worth of honey. After the customer had gone, the old woman's granddaughter trembled and said the woman had looked exactly like the young peasant wife who had recently died.

The very next day the same young woman came again, asking for more honey. To a question from the proprietress, she answered: "It's for my baby, for I have no milk."

117

At a signal from her grandmother, the little girl followed the young woman with her eyes and saw her disappear in the direction of her tomb.

The shopkeeper advised the husband of this strange event. Next day, going to get some water, he stopped at the straw hut and waited. Toward evening, observing his wife approach, he thrust himself in front of her and spoke to her. She appeared not to hear him, and, lowering her head, she ran away. He hastened in pursuit, but she suddenly disappeared completely.

Dissolved in tears, the husband ran like a crazy man to the tomb and threw himself against it with cries of despair. He remained there, motionless and prostrate, while his tears continued to flow.

Then suddenly he thought he heard a child's cries coming from the tomb. He cupped his ear to the stone and heard the cries distinctly.

He ran to his home, returned with a spade, and began to dig down to the coffin. When he opened it, he saw an infant boy lying on the stomach of his dead mother and moving feebly. On the corners of his mouth, the infant bore traces of honey. The woman's body was cold but unblemished, and it seemed to her husband that her serene, still face was almost smiling, rather than painfully contracted as it had been at the time of her death.

The young father carried the child back to his house. Then the neighbors helped him to reclose the coffin and the tomb.

In the village the father sought some woman willing to nurse his son. But everyone was afraid and stole away from him when he approached. For a time he had to feed the baby on rice gruel, but gradually the compassionate hearts of his neighbors overcame some of their fears, and after several days one of the neighborhood women volunteered to serve as a wet nurse.

The child grew up normally from that time, and his subsequent life revealed nothing out of the ordinary at all.

As for the mother, no one ever saw her again. Her husband revisited the tomb a number of times, but always found nothing. And even though he also went periodically to the whole area she had traversed, including the straw hut of the merchant, his wife never appeared before him again.

Many times he went to the pagoda to pray for his wife's return, sometimes even spending the whole night there in prayer. But all was in vain: he never saw her again, not even in his dreams.

It might be assumed that the poor wife's strength and determination had sustained her even beyond the grave, but only to the point where she could fulfill her destiny by giving birth to her son and feeding him for the first few days. Such efforts of themselves must have so exhausted her that the remnants of life that customarily permit dead spirits to visit the sleep of the living for some time were, in her case, no longer present.

The Game of Chess in the Mountains

THE FATHER OF HIEN THE PIOUS was a woodcutter. One day in the forest he was seized by a tiger and carried away. From that day on, he was never seen again.

Ever since that dreadful time the boy had helped his mother earn a meager living for themselves and the younger children of the family. Hien was strong for his years, fortunately, and very brave, so that already he could hew as much wood as a grown man. His mother, prematurely worn out, congratulated herself on being able to toil a little less now. She continued to take on dressmaking tasks, but she was no longer obliged to go out to work at the homes of other people, doing the hardest and dreariest chores.

❖   ❖   ❖

One winter evening, three long years after his father's disappearance, Hien was returning home through the forest, heavily loaded. Suddenly he noticed a human form stretched out motionless at the edge of the path. Hien put down his load and bent over the stricken person. It was an old man, still breathing, but very feebly. Hien the Pious put the old man on his back and carried him to his straw hut. There neither his mother nor he spared themselves in giving the sick man the best care they could command. They had the joy of seeing him revive, and they kept him in their home to await full recovery, depriving themselves for his sake, without any notion of earning reward for their charity.

One evening the old man said to Hien: "Before leaving you, I want to give you some evidence of my gratitude. I happen to know that this very year your name is inscribed in the Book of the Dead, but I am going to show you a way in which you can be saved from that fate. Pay very close attention to what I tell you.

"On the very first day of next month, you should set out early, carrying a calabash of wine and two cups. After crossing the forest, continue in the direction of the rising sun until you reach the edge of a lake with very blue water. Then climb the mountain there, pass to the left of a waterfall, and not far from the summit of the mountain you will come upon two old men playing a game of chess. Don't make any sound, but approach them and stand close; when they ask you for something to drink, pour them out some of your wine. You must wait until they have completely finished their game before you address your request to them."

The next morning the guest had disappeared.

✦　✦　✦

On the first day of the following month, well before dawn, Hien set out on his journey, his calabash of wine suspended on his back and his two cups well wrapped.

After he had passed through the forest he followed a road that was new to him. The sun was high in the vault of the sky when he reached a lake whose waters were of a deep blue. Deep in the woods covering the sides of the mountain he could hear the songs of unknown birds resounding marvelously in the clear air, an air incredibly brisk and pure, like sharp wine. He stopped to listen to the birds. In the intervals of silence he heard the sound of a distant waterfall. He proceeded then in the direction of this sound, left the waterfall on his right, and soon found himself on the border of a woods, looking at a magnificent landscape of mountains bathed in translucent light.

Here, in a well-situated spot under a large pine tree, two old men were seated, legs crossed, on either side of a smooth stone table. Approaching noiselessly, Hien got a good view of their handsome faces, which shone ruddily despite numerous wrinkles. The old men played on in silence, calculating their moves reflectively. Each time that they stooped a bit to advance a piece, the points of their long white beards skimmed the red lines of the board that was marked out on the stone surface.

Hien also noticed that each man had beside him a large closed book. He stood beside them motionless for a moment.

Then one of the old men, without moving his eyes from the board, commanded as to a servant: "Some drink!"

Hien hastened to unwrap his cups and fill them. Then he placed them within reach of the players' hands. The men, still absorbed in the game, emptied the cups.

Three times this little act was repeated. Finally the game ended, and the winner raised his eyes for the first time.

At the same moment Hien made obeisance, prostrated himself, his forehead to the ground, saying: "Gracious Spirit, spare me, out of pity for my mother, who is old and feeble. Grant me still a few years of life, time enough for my younger brothers to become big and strong enough to replace me at her side."

The old men leaned toward each other and murmured. One of them opened his book, picked up his brush, and corrected a character. Then he said to Hien: "You surprised us by offering us your drink. What is more important, you are a good son, and you have saved a man's life. Your own life is therefore lengthened now to a hundred years."

Hien, still prostrate, had not had time to utter his thanks to the spirits when he felt a small puff of wind pass over his head. He arose and saw that the two sides of the stone chessboard were now empty. Nothing remained except the two wine cups and the calabash.

He started back on the road to his home, running. Joy overflowed from his heart, but he did not dare to tell anyone, not even his mother, what had befallen him.

Later on, he returned to the mountain. He found the lake again without too much difficulty, then the woods with the waterfall. But the waters of the lake seemed not so blue, the air of the woods held no birdsong, and in the silence the waterfall roared alone. Farther off, the same pine tree extended its shade over a rough stone, where Hien sought in vain the red markings of the spirits' chessboard.

The Scholar and the Thieves

AN AGED SCHOLAR, CHILDLESS and without funds, wandered from village to village seeking to give lessons in order to earn a meager living.

One night, half dead of hunger and fatigue, the poor man found himself stranded in the open countryside, with only a rude and abandoned straw hut for shelter. He entered it, curled up in a corner, covered himself with straw, and promptly dozed off from weakness and exhaustion.

In the middle of the night he awakened with a start. He could hear people entering the hut and putting down burdens of some kind. When the intruders lighted a torch, the scholar could see several men whose faces were daubed with soot. Armed with pikes and knives, these fierce-looking men were carrying burning incense. From sacks and cases flung to the floor tumbled an array of copper utensils: cooking pots, trays, basins, and other objects. This was clearly a band of robbers carrying off its plunder.

The old man guarded against making a move, so as not to give his presence away. Some of the robbers approached quite close to where he lay, but none paid any attention to the heap of rags and straw in the corner.

Without losing much time, the robber band started to fix something to eat. Peering from his dark corner across the straw stalks concealing him, the scholar could see a huge pot of rice, other stolen foods, and even a jug of rice wine. He began to suffer the tortures of the famished at the noises made by the thieves when they fell to eating and drinking.

Suddenly one of the gang, his mouth crammed with food, announced that he was cold. Looking for something with which to make a fire, he came upon a pile of straw. Scarcely had he touched it than he jumped back, crying out: "Watch out, people! There's somebody in here!"

All his companions quickly jumped up, seizing their weapons, and encircled the pile—from which emerged the poor old scholar, saying humbly: "I am only a teacher of calligraphy."

Immediately there was a general burst of relieved laughter. "What are you doing here?" asked the chief of the robber band.

The scholar straightened his turban before replying. Then he told the group his story of poverty and homelessness. The robber chief, despite his calling, had had some education, and he had retained the traditional respect for learning and for old age. So he suggested that the teacher accept him, the robber, as his protector.

But the old man, with gentle dignity, refused.

However, he was so close to the end of his strength that he had momentary difficulty in standing upright. He suddenly tottered and fell backward. The thieves then poured a little rice wine between his lips, and he soon came to himself again. Then the men brought him a bowl of rice and some dried meat. But the scholar would not touch the food.

Thinking the old man was merely too weak to serve himself, the leader squatted down beside him, and, prying open the teacher's jaws, placed a little rice in his mouth.

But the scholar shook his head and spat out the grains on the ground.

"It is far better to die of hunger," said he, "than to eat rice stolen from other people."

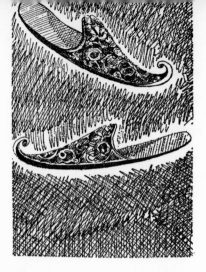

A Willow Wand and a Brocade Slipper

ONCE UPON A VERY LONG TIME ago, a man who had lost his wife lived alone with his little girl Tam. But, after a lengthy period of mourning, he remarried; and his new wife was extremely unkind to her stepdaughter, neglecting her and mistreating her, often to the point of flogging her and then sending her to bed hungry, without even a bowl of rice or noodles.

Matters grew even worse after a baby girl was born to the new wife. This child was named Cam, and her mother adored her as much as she hated Tam. The woman told her husband many falsehoods about Tam; and when she had convinced him that his daughter had been disobedient, then she could say to Tam: "Go stay in the kitchen and look after yourself, you naughty girl!"

So except when she was working Tam spent most of her time in a dirty corner of the kitchen. At night she was given a torn mat and ragged sheet as bed and cover.

And while Cam played happily all day with her mother, Tam had to do all the hard work. She had to scrub floors, cut wood, feed the animals, cook, and wash clothes. Her poor little hands became rough and blistered, but she bore the pain without complaint. Sometimes she had to go far into the forest to gather wood or to draw water from deep wells or distant springs. Thus did poor little Tam work and work all day every day, until her skin became swarthy and her hair matted and tangled.

One day, looking down at herself in the water of a spring, Tam was frightened to realize how dark and ugly she had become. Taking some water in the hollow of her hand, she rubbed it over her face and looked again. Her soft white skin had reappeared, and Tam looked very pretty indeed.

When Tam returned home, her cruel stepmother also noticed this

126

loveliness. Tam was far prettier than her own daughter Cam. So her resentment became greater than ever.

One day the mother asked Tam and Cam to go together to the village pond to catch fish. She said to the girls: "If you return without any fish, you'll be punished properly and sent to bed without supper."

But Tam knew that these words were intended for her alone. So she did her very best, and by the end of the afternoon she had a basket full of nice plump fish. Cam, meantime, had passed the hours frolicking and picking flowers in a nearby meadow where water buffalo were grazing.

When the sun was setting and it was time to leave, Cam looked at her own empty basket and had a bright idea. "Sister," said she, "your hair is covered with mud. Why don't you take time to wash it in the pond?"

Tam decided to do as Cam suggested. But, while she was out in the water, bent over, Cam dumped all the fish from her sister's basket into her own, and then went off home. When Tam realized what had happened, she wept bitterly.

Suddenly the Goddess of Mercy, gentle and sweet and tender, appeared before her, gowned in a beautiful azure tunic. "My dear child," said she softly, "what is troubling you?"

Tam told the apparition of her misfortune. But the goddess consoled her in a voice like muted bells. "Your bad luck will soon be ended," said she. "Have confidence in me. Now, look in your basket again. What do you see there?"

Tam peered down into the basket and saw lying there one fish, a beautiful red-gold carp. The Goddess of Mercy told Tam to carry the carp home, put it in the well there, and feed it three times each day.

Tam thanked her heavenly benefactress and did as she was told. But her stepmother soon observed this daily routine. So one day she ordered Tam to go to a far-distant spring to fetch water. While the child was away, the mother caught the carp in the well, killed, cooked, and ate it!

When Tam returned home she went to the well to feed her fish, calling out to him when she couldn't see him; but of course he never appeared. Once again the poor girl wept, inconsolably. But once again the tender Goddess of Mercy appeared to her, saying: "Be comforted, my child, and cease your crying. Try to find the bones of your fish and bury them in the ground beneath your sleeping mat. Then, whenever you want anything, make a request to the bones and almost certainly it will be granted."

Tam found the bones after a long search; they were buried in a heap of refuse. Once found, she cleaned them carefully, wrapped them, and buried them neatly, as the goddess had instructed. When she needed something, she asked the bones softly and nicely, and as a result, she accumulated some lovely dresses in the *ao-dai* style, a gold chain, and a golden disk in the shape of an ancient coin.

She thought that when time for the Mid-Autumn Festival came she could dress in this new finery and attend it like a real lady. But just at that time the stepmother commanded Tam to remain at home and sort out the black and green beans which the stepmother had mixed up in two large baskets. Then the mother took Cam, dressed in her best, and went off to the festival celebrations.

Tam lifted her tear-filled eyes and prayed: "Benevolent Goddess of Mercy, please help me!"

At once the goddess reappeared, and with her magic green willow branch turned a number of little flies into ricebirds. These ricebirds quickly sorted the beans for Tam. Then, after looking at Tam's new gowns and deciding she needed something even more splendid, the goddess, with another wave of her willow wand, created a resplendent and glittering blue and silver robe, and the most beautiful pair of matching brocade slippers that had ever been seen.

Tam dressed herself carefully in this gorgeous clothing and adorned herself with the golden chain and disk. Then, looking for all the world like a true princess, off she went to the festival.

Cam and her mother were both surprised and jealous to see this beautiful stranger arrive and capture everyone's attention. Cam turned to her mother and spoke under her breath: "Doesn't that fine lady look strangely like Tam?"

Tam saw them whispering to each other and looking in her direction, and she became frightened. Turning quickly, she fled away. Her hurry was so great that she lost one of the beautiful slippers, which was picked up by a soldier of the guard and turned over to the king.

The king examined the slipper carefully and declared that he had never before seen such a work of art and that he must meet its owner. He had all the ladies of the court try the slipper on, but it was too tiny to fit any of them. Then the king ordered all the noblewomen of the kingdom to try it, but neither would it fit any of them. Finally word was sent out everywhere that whoever had a foot to fit that slipper would be made a lady of the court.

In due time Tam had a chance to try on the slipper, which naturally fitted her to perfection. She was then dressed once more in her blue and

silver gown, her golden jewelry, and the brocade slippers, and brought to the court. The king fell promptly in love with beautiful Tam, made her his queen, and together they lived ever afterward an unbelievably brilliant and happy life.

As for the cruel stepmother and her daughter Cam, they became so enraged at Tam's good fortune that they burst blood vessels and died.

It never does to become so jealous, does it?

The Raven's Magic Gem

A PAIR OF RAVENS HAD BUILT their nest in the top of a tall flame tree, and in it were four nestlings. It had been an unseasonable spring, and the mother raven was sick with cold and exhaustion. The baby ravens, too, were cold and very, very hungry.

"Tweet! Tweet!" peeped the four little ones to their shiny-feathered father, who sat forlornly on a nearby branch. "We feel so hungry, Father! Can't you find us something to eat, even one fat juicy caterpillar that we could share?"

Poor Father Raven, who loved his wife and children very much indeed, was quite distraught. With an anxious look behind at the nest, he flew away yet again in his ceaseless but largely unsuccessful search for food for his frail, shivering offspring. Far, far, far over the fields he flew; but his search was unrewarded until, almost ready to give up in despair, he caught sight of the figure of a young boy lying motionless in some tall elephant grass at the edge of a meadow.

"That boy isn't making a move," thought Mr. Raven. "He is most certainly dead. Alas, alack! Still, I can peck out his eyes and fetch them to my hungry children. He will have no more use for them, but they will be something for the babies' stomachs."

And so he swooped low to snatch the boy's eyes.

But the boy was not really dead at all. He was a buffalo-boy, lying on the ground in total dejection because he had just lost the single buffalo that was his charge. His master had become so hopelessly entangled in debt that one of his impatient creditors had seized the animal in payment. Now the boy lay despairingly on the ground, not knowing where to go or what to do. He feared his master's rage, and longed only to die and escape a world of suffering and disappointment.

131

When he noticed the raven flying so close to him, the lad sat up, seized the bird, and said: "There now, you wicked bird, what are you trying to do, peck out my eyes? Well, I've caught you instead, and I just think I'll wring your neck!"

The raven was frightened, thinking of his sick wife and hungry children left alone in a hostile world. "Croak, croak!" croaked he. "I beseech you, young master, let me go! My wife is sick in our nest, our children starving. I was only seeking food for them and would never have approached you if I hadn't believed you dead. Do set me free!"

The buffalo-boy was really tenderhearted, so, moved by this plea, he let the raven go. But before flying off, the bird said: "You have done me and my family a great kindness. Now I want to do something to convince you of my gratitude."

Whereupon he spat out a large and glittering jewel which he presented to the boy. The latter most happily accepted it, as you can well imagine.

"This is a very special, very precious gem," said the raven. "It has magic power, the power to grant you whatever you may wish for." And croaking happily, the raven circled the boy, then headed up into the sky and was soon lost to sight.

"My!" exclaimed the boy. "What a strange thing! How I do wish I had a buffalo to take to my master!" No sooner were these words out of his mouth than a large gray buffalo stood before the boy's startled eyes. Seizing the rope around the animal's neck, the boy lost no time in guiding the buffalo back to his overjoyed master.

Once that was accomplished, the buffalo-boy gave up his job, for he was weary of putting up with the master's bad temper and evil ways.

The boy went home and sat down, thinking: "Wouldn't it be fine if I had a large house in a beautiful garden!"

In the twinkling of an eye, the boy's surroundings were changed. He sat now in a magnificent villa, from whose long windows he could look out upon a sun-drenched, flower-filled garden, quite the most beautiful he had ever seen. While he stood looking amazedly about and admiring everything he saw, smartly uniformed servants came to the door to invite their young master into the dining salon, where a splendid banquet was spread. While he tasted the many fine dishes, his new attendants scurried about to anticipate his every desire.

Next, they showed him to a handsome bedchamber where a wardrobe was stocked with elegant clothing, all of which fitted him to perfection. Now the boy felt both rich and important—but still, did he possess all

that he might? Obviously not. Gazing deep into the gem, which he cradled in his hand, the young man wished once again: "Would that I possessed many hectares of rich rice paddy!"

As the words fell from his lips, all the marshland in the area of his home turned into emerald-green rice fields surrounded by lush meadows in which many-colored butterflies hovered and nightingales sang.

Now, truly, the boy seemed to lack nothing to complete the perfection of his life. But he was growing up, and one day he experienced a new sensation—loneliness. Once again, then, he made a wish: "How nice it would be if a beautiful and graceful young lady could become my wife, to give me companionship and share all this joy!"

Immediately the very handsomest young girl in the countryside came to him as a bride. Looking at her large dark eyes, her smooth dark brows, and her lovely, fair complexion, the young man felt that now, certainly, his happiness was complete.

As for the new bride, she found her young husband very agreeable, and life in this magnificent home totally pleasant. But she was a dutiful, loving daughter also and she couldn't help wanting her parents to share in this abundance. So she prodded from her husband the secret of his wealth. Foolishly in love, he could deny her nothing.

But one day when he was out inspecting his rice fields, his wife stole the magic gem and carried it secretly to her parents' home.

When the young husband returned and realized his double loss, his state of mind became frantic. Helplessly, he wept.

Then the good Lord Buddha appeared before him, floating on a lotus, and said, extending his hands: "My son, behold two magic flowers which I give you. One is white, the other red. Take them both to the home of your parents-in-law. Strange things will happen when the white flower is shown. Your parents-in-law will probably appeal to you for help. Then the red flower will set everything to rights. All will be well in the end. Go now."

Of course the young man did exactly as Lord Buddha told him.

Placed before the gate of the wife's former home, the white flower emitted a sweet, rather exotic fragrance, so rare indeed that everyone in the house came out to sniff it. But lo and behold! In a trice their noses became exceedingly long, as long as an elephant's trunk! Their neighbors saw this phenomenon and doubled up with laughter.

The wife's father wailed: "Heavens above, what is our wrongdoing, that such a curse should be laid upon us?"

"I can tell you," responded the son-in-law. "It's because your daugh-